Clairvoyant

Clairvoyant

Copyright © 2025 by Samantha Alis

This is a work of fiction. Any resemblance to actual events, places, incidents, or persons, living or dead, is coincidental.

All rights reserved.

Published in the United States by Samantha Alis. For inquiries, please visit the author's website at: https://authorsamanthaalis.my.canva.site/

Cover design by Vaish (@canvaish)

Interior design by MG (@mgsdesiigns)

Edited by Amanda Van Dahm (@vandahm_edits)

eBook 979-8-9914112-3-3

Paperback 979-8-9914112-2-6

No part of this book has been created using Generative AI. The author does not consent for her works to be utilized in any form of machine learning training.

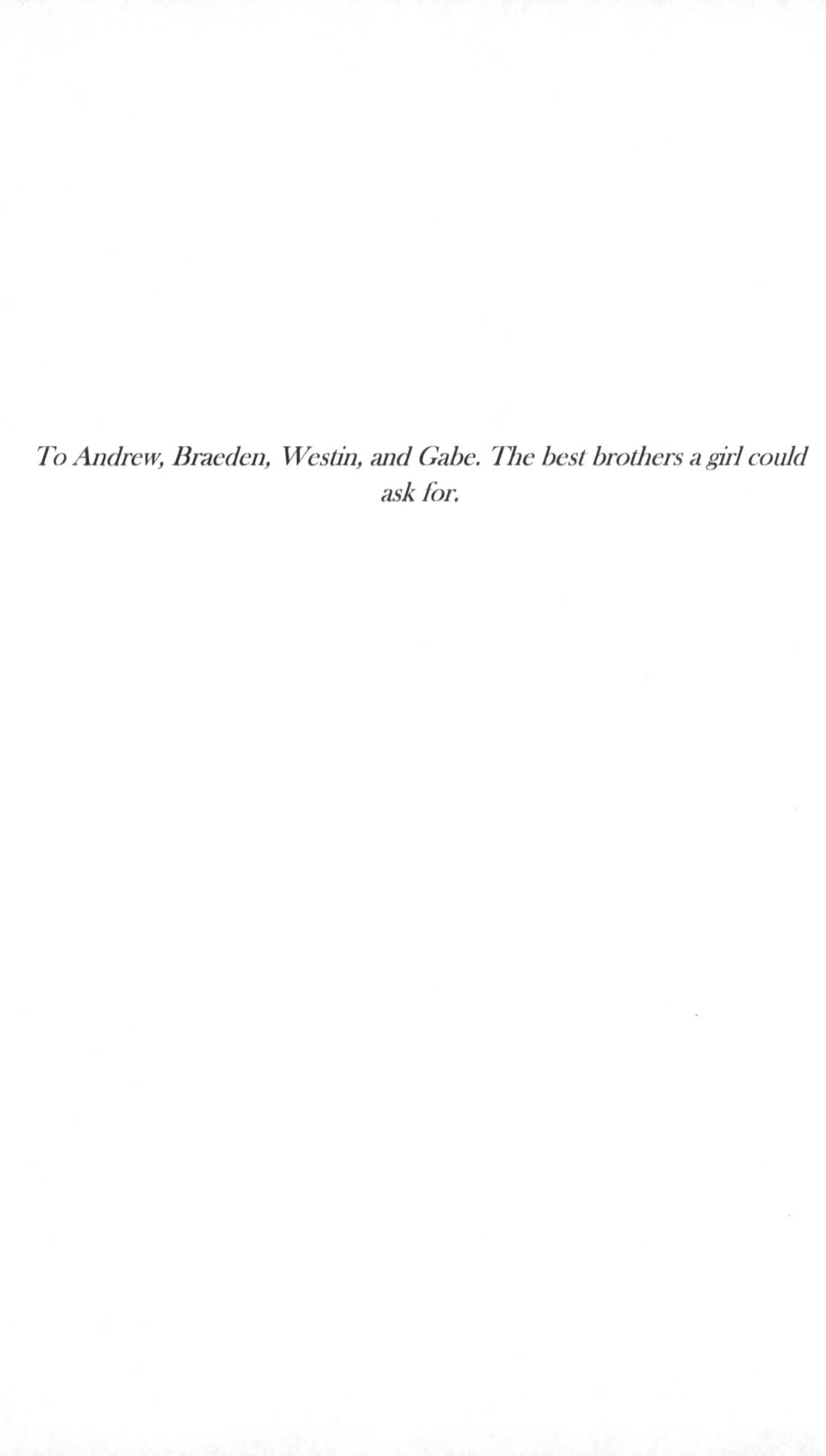

To Andrew, Braeden, Westin, and Gabe. The best brothers a girl could ask for.

Content Warnings

Clairvoyant is a paranormal mystery where depictions of violence take place on the page. The story contains: murder, mentions of suicide, mentions of dismemberment, mentions of abuse.

A single leather boot clings to her calf to perch beneath her right knee. Her other foot is bare—pale in the moonlight and the icy glimmer of frost among strewn leaves.

Deep cuts and oblong bruises invade her skin. Dark, stringy hair grips her dirty scalp in clumps. She swipes strands from her eyes.

Panting breaths frost the air as she twirls around, the sleeves of brown and yellow flannel falling from bare shoulders.

My heart flutters and falls. She's long gone. There's nothing to be done.

Her eyes widen and mist in the moonlight streaming through a thick canopy of pine needles overhead. A scream rips from her throat, but it's hoarse and weak.

She cries as she stumbles away from me. The soles of her feet are scarred and pink. One of her big toenails is missing, ripped clean off with no remnants to cling to the fleshy underside.

My hiking boots crunch after her, swallowing her light trodden path from before. My breath is loud and languid. I've done this before. I must have.

My heart beats steadily. I'm not worried about her escape. She won't get far. No help will come. Her body will never be found.

The girl squeaks out a plea before falling forward, twisting the leather around her leg in a corkscrew. Pink-tinged saliva coats her teeth as a raspy wail leaves her lips. "I won't tell. I promise I won't tell. I'll leave town. Nobody will know. Nobody will know anything."

She sounds young. Her voice is high pitched and broken, like she sucked on a small dose of helium.

Wet mud squelches under my boots, slowing me slightly, as it tries to keep my feet glued to the forest floor.

I'm suddenly aware of cold metal in my hand. Thick, blunt, and heavy.

I wish I could close my eyes. I don't like this part.

I stride forward, a laugh tickling my throat. I've done this a lot. I'm not nervous, or apprehensive. I'm excited. Hunger bloats my belly. The second I'm finished with her I'll find another and another and another. None will satiate my appetite.

A wide smile makes my cheeks ache as I raise my arm and hit her with my weapon.

It looks like a meat tenderizer. Small studs poke out of a heavy, metal square. It connects with her face, her shoulders, her arms, her stomach.

Tufts of steam rise from her body once I'm finished.

I drop the weapon by my feet and stalk back into the darkness I emerged from.

Her body is out in the open for any explorer, hiker, or camper to find if they wander too far from any marked paths. I don't bother to wipe fingerprints off my discarded weapon or scrub the blood from my clothing and shoes.

Yes. I've done this before.

I'm ripped from the vision with a jolt and spindly fingers tapping my right shoulder.

An older woman with a soft smile and crinkles around her brown eyes covers her mouth with her hand. "I'm sorry to startle you, dear. I only wanted to ask if I could sit beside you."

My stomach sloshes around dissolving orange juice and about six different drugs ranging from ones meant to relax the body to antipsychotics. I squeeze my hands into two small fists and release them to abate the tremors.

Bodies of all sizes tucked into muted peacoats and colorful windbreakers crowd the cross-country charter bus.

Drops of rain trail down the window beside me. Fog slowly disbands from the glass where I must have pressed my head and looked out to the forest that triggered my vision. My stomach lurches again. That vision. That girl. She looked so scared. She died somewhere out there. A violent, bloody, awful death.

"Excuse me," the woman says again, timid this time. I look unstable, I'm sure. Sweat plasters dark hair to my forehead and neck. My navy blue sweatshirt and matching sweatpants paint a very clear picture of where I've traveled from. My tennis shoes are the only item of clothing that don't outright scream: *She's crazy! She's been institutionalized!*

"Where are we?" It's the first time I've spoken more than a single-word sentence in weeks. The sound of my own voice, scratchy and unused, even catches me off guard. The woman leans away from my two-seat row and peers around the rest of the bus. Nobody wants to get stuck sitting beside the weird girl across state lines.

I clear my throat and try again. "Where are we?"

"Baneberry Grove, dear."

My stop. Time flies when you're temporarily stuffed in the skin of a killer.

"You can have the whole row." I slide my duffle bag from under my seat and stand in the narrow aisle. Relief floods the woman's face. She plops down in the aisle seat and leans away from the air I once occupied.

I'm sure the Delilah I once was, months ago, would do anything to plead with this woman, to convince her I'm not crazy. I'm sweet and kind and thoughtful and every other pleasant adjective I could think of on a whim. But I don't really care anymore. I'll never see her again. She'll probably forget about me once her trip starts and she's hundreds of miles from this town. Nobody on this bus will remember me.

Just like no one will remember the girl in the woods.

I shake the thought from my head. I can't think about that. I don't think about those things anymore.

A shiver races down my spine and across my arms, drawing up translucent hairs and pinprick-sized bumps of flesh. They offered me a blanket before I left. It was the same near-midnight blue as my clothing and had the facility name embroidered across one corner in ugly block print. I didn't need another reminder I'd spent four weeks of my life locked behind white brick walls, downing multicolored pills, and pretending the images in my head were figments of my imagination instead of past horrific events.

The bus station is nearly empty. The next pickup isn't due until noon according to glowing signs screwed into every wall. It is—I count several weeks on my fingers—the beginning of August. Summer break is still in full swing for many.

A janitor sweeps away crumpled brown napkins and rain-soaked leaves into a dustpan—preparing for the next chaotic mess of travelers.

I provide a polite smile to him after accidentally stepping on an empty styrofoam coffee cup and splitting it into a pile of gummy pieces. He only glances at me once before making a beeline to the backroom. This outfit acts as a deterrent for any social interaction, I see.

A handful of fluffy yellow popcorn pelts the back of my head.

"Don't tell me you already forgot what I look like."

A smile—a real one this time—breaks my stoic composure. Conner, my big brother. By twenty-seven minutes.

He tosses another handful of popcorn as I turn around. Several pieces stick to the collar of my shirt and the rest rain around me, creating a ritualistic looking circle. I raise an eyebrow. "You gonna clean that up?"

He shrugs and stuffs a handful into his mouth. "The birds will."

"We're indoors." I can't help but chuckle. I've missed him.

He loops an arm around my shoulder in a half-hug as he drags me from the station. "Well then, I guess they'll have to be brave and find a way inside." He taps the half-empty paper bag against my arm. I shake my head. The pills make me too sick for solids until at least two in the afternoon.

"The fair is in town," Conner says with a full mouth.

Outside, we're greeted by a chill breeze and the smell of soil soaking up prior raindrops. Vivid green flourishes all around us. Dense trees circle the building, and thick reeds sway along the trunks. "They've really upped their game this year, Lilah. I'm telling you, even John looked like he was having fun on the new tilt-a-whirl. It goes upside down now. Have you ever spun upside down? Because you haven't experienced life until then."

"Upside down, huh?" Truthfully, that sounds awful. Old Delilah would have forced Conner and John to ride something like that over and over until at least one of us threw up. But new Delilah has no desire for an adrenaline rush or excessive spinning of any kind. New Delilah is mellow, calm, and trying to be boring. New Delilah is normal.

"Yeah and the food! You gotta try the food. Just try one piece, please. They seasoned it this year. And not with salt, but with little orange and red flakes. It's spicy and sweet all at the same time."

I pop a piece of popcorn into my mouth from the collar of my shirt. It is spicy and sweet, and if it were three in the afternoon, I might have appreciated it more, but as of right now all I want to do is spit it out on the sidewalk.

Conner must notice my face, because he tucks the nearly empty bag into his back pocket. "Don't worry. They have way more than just popcorn. We can find something you'll enjoy."

I'm surprised Conner didn't bring the truck to pick me up. I wonder if this is a ploy set up by our father. One to get me talking, revealing the thoughts and intricacies hidden away in my mind.

Conner releases me from his arm to tug the duffle bag from my hand. "I'm not gonna go through it if that's what you're so worried about." Dimples indent his cheeks, molding his jaw from square to boyishly chubby for half a second.

I release the straps and rub the ache of their digging from my palms. I hadn't realized I was holding it so tightly. "Sorry. I think I'm nervous."

"Nervous about what?"

I stop walking to point up the hill to our house. It's large, white, and two-stories tall with a porch wrapping around the bottom floor. Two figures in rocking chairs raise their heads when they see me. The larger one stands while the smaller one adjusts the glasses set on his nose and leans into a book on his lap.

"He was only trying to help," Conner says, waving to our father as he makes his way down the path.

"Don't take his side." I don't mean to sound so gruff, but I'm still regaining strength in my voice, and it comes out like a snarl.

"There are no sides, Lilah."

Our father stops in front of me. The tips of his shined dress shoes somehow avoided picking up a single speck of dirt on his journey down the muddy walk. He extends his arms. "Welcome home."

I hesitate for only a moment before I stride past him with a grumbled thank you.

Conner and our father work their way back up to the house as I nod to acknowledge John, my younger brother by fifteen minutes, as he continues to study whatever subject interests him nowadays. He follows me inside and heads for the kitchen. I take the stairs that wrap around the middle of the house in a square shape to my room.

It's been recently cleaned. Or maybe it was cleaned after the incident and has sat empty for the last four weeks. Either way, it looks a lot better than last time I was here.

My clothes are precisely folded and put away. My bed is made up with new blankets, green ones with little pink and yellow flowers dotted across the fabric. I can't be sure, but I think they might be dahlias.

A pang of guilt squeezes my heart. A gift bag sits on my desk that faces the window and the dense cluster of trees that surround our property. A card is propped up beside it, decorated with heart-shaped balloons and rainbow confetti. I don't need to open it to know what's inside. Heartfelt, loving notes from my brothers, a sentence about my return from our father. Possibly some cash, or tickets to the fair, or some other fun thing meant to lift my spirits.

My spirits were lifted when I checked out of the mental health institution two towns over. Then the reality of my situation—my life—hit me in the face like a meat tenderizer. The visions would never stop. I would never be free. And I could never save anybody.

Through the droplets clinging to my bedroom window, I watch Conner and our father standing side by side, gazing out at the main road, talking amongst themselves. Our father shakes his head and Conner pats him on the back.

A quiet ping draws my attention. I smile and leap onto my bed and tear my cell phone from the charging station on the bedside table. The notifications aren't from anyone in particular, future colleges, town events, social media pages about fuzzy animals and gardening. It looks like someone dug deep into my phone while I was gone and removed all the articles I archived about cold cases and other unsolved crimes. A parental advisory warning pops up on the screen when I open a new tab. Blocked phrases include, but are not limited to, *dead, missing, buried, murdered, killed, kidnapped,* and *attacked.*

Our father doesn't need to worry. I won't be searching for any of those phrases. I'm finished with my investigations. My visions are just that: visions. They aren't a call to action. They won't hurt me if I ignore them, so ignore them I will. Old Delilah nearly lost her life trying to save everyone. New Delilah would not make the same mistake. New Delilah takes antipsychotics and turns the other cheek.

I lift my head at a soft knock on my open bedroom door. John's eyes drift from me to the phone in my hand. A thick book is tucked under his arm. I can only read half the title: "-1875."

"How are you?" he asks. John's voice is flat, the theory of intonation lost on him. Yet, I know he is concerned for me because he made the effort to check on me.

I shrug. Truthfully, my emotions are as flat as my brother's voice. My ride home was a battle between hope and despair. I'm free, that much is a point for positivity. Yet am I really free if visions plague my days?

"Did you open your gift?" he asks. When people meet my brother for the first time, they struggle to understand what he says. John is articulate, every word perfectly pronounced, but his lack of inflection makes everything sound like a statement—a final proclamation.

"Not yet."

"You won't like it." His eyes remain trained on the gift.

I roll off the bed and grab the bag, bringing it to John. "You can have it then."

"I won't like it either."

I remove glittery, light pink paper from the top to drop on the polished, dark wood beneath my feet. I reach inside and my fingers settle around a cardstock paper. I bring it out and hold it up to my face. It's an invitation to the sheriff's re-election gala coming up in less than two weeks.

My heart feels heavy, like it should drop into my stomach and down to my feet from the weight. Our father attends these things regularly, and I'm always his plus one. I like—*liked*—the music, the food, the people. It's the only time I do my hair, pinned up with shining, studded pins, do my makeup to appear like a different person, wear a glamorous dress I wouldn't normally wear. The last time I went to one was a week before I left. A charity gala to raise funds for the fire department. I hadn't fully enjoyed the event like I normally would. Details of another gruesome case I couldn't solve stuffed my mind like wadded tissue paper.

I toss the gift bag back on the desk and turn the invitation over in my hands.

John turns from the room. "I told him you wouldn't like it," he says as he disappears down the hall.

If things are going to be different—if I'm going to be different—I can't fall into the same routines. I can't attend galas with our father, conversing with the intention of finding a lead. I can't let visions consume my thoughts. I can't prioritize other people's needs over my own.

I crumple the invitation into a ball and toss it on the desk alongside the bag. I'm different now. I have to be to survive.

The fair is loud and bright, the exact opposite of what I need right now. But when Conner suggested it over an awkward and silent lunch of egg salad sandwiches and potato chips, and our father politely dismissed the idea, I had to chirp up and say it sounded excellent. The sooner I pushed myself back into the normal family routine—the better.

I immediately regret my decision the second we exit the car. The ruckus of overexcited voices meld with the bright flashing lights of carnival rides—held down by bricks and trembling bolts—blurring my vision and sending my heartbeat pounding in my ears. I clamp my teeth together and squeeze my eyes shut.

Crowds aren't normally an issue, at least they hadn't been. Until the incident. Now breathing is all I can do to keep myself grounded and from hurling myself into the backseat of the car and demanding a ride home.

A hand rests on my shoulder. It feels warm and clammy through the fabric of my shirt. Our father lowers his voice so only I can hear his question. "Are you sure you want to go tonight? There's no shame in trying again later."

I open my eyes to meet his.

Is it sharks that smell fear? Or maybe bears? Mountain lions? I'll have to ask John which one. Our father is like a fear-smelling animal. His nose twitches at the scent I give off, the reek of apprehension.

He can smell my fear, but I can't let him believe it. If I want to remain here with my brothers, not locked away, I need to show my successful rehabilitation. If I give him any reason to believe I'm not ready to be here, he might send me back. I can't go back. I can't.

"Positive! Looks fun. Can't wait to ride everything and try all the new food." I plaster the fakest grin I can muster onto my face. It feels like a plastic party store mask—itchy and hot. Our father nods once before heading toward the fair.

Our first stop is a corn dog stand recommended by Conner. Traditional batter is abandoned to make room for crushed chips or fried pickles. I refuse a bite of Conner's stuffed salsa dog and end up ordering a cup of plain minis that I give to John after only popping one greasy oval in my mouth.

Conner leads us around like an overexcited tour guide, pointing out attractions he recommends and other food stands that serve unique concoctions. I spend the tour with my eyes down, stepping on confetti stamped into trampled grass. Our father hangs toward the back of our trio—several paces away—hands in his pockets, watching us...me mostly.

"Hello," Conner waves his hand in front of my face, and I lift my head up. "Did you hear me?"

"Um...which part?"

Conner raises a brow. "Any of it?"

I dig the tip of my shoe into the grass, unearthing damp dirt underneath. "Not really. I'm sorry."

Conner plants a smile on his face. "That's alright. I was rambling anyway. Anything here interest you?"

I finally gaze up at the fair surrounding me. Bright, flashing red and white lights force me to squint. The ride nearest to us is some kind of miniature Ferris wheel that goes up and down at a stomach-clenching angle. A child with blue sugar stuck to his fingers and chin leans over the railing of his seat to release a stream of half-digested cotton candy.

I turn away as my stomach twists. "I'll be honest, I don't think I can handle any of these rides. Not right now."

Conner does his best to keep that smile on his face to reassure me, but I see a slight falter. The edges of his lips twitch as he holds them up.

"What about the funhouse?" John says.

"Man, nobody wants to go to the funhouse. The entire attraction is just walking around and looking at things," Conner says. "It's basically a museum."

"I didn't say you have to come." John removes his glasses to wipe the lenses against the hem of his polo.

"Start riding the fun rides. We won't be gone long." I share a polite smile with my older brother. I can't help but feel guilty. He's been looking forward to taking me to the fair, and so far I've only turned down his ideas while here.

John leads me to the edge of the fair, where flashing lights flicker, overheated bulbs stuttering to stay alive. Grass gives way to dry, packed dirt. The noise of happy squeals and buzzing carnival games doesn't quite reach here, and my shoulders tense at the vacuum of sound.

Instead of looking forward, I watch my brother's long strides. As long as he stays in my sight, I know I'm here—in this moment—and not on the brink of witnessing, experiencing, or committing another murder. I squeeze my hands into fists. It's either that or I reach out and clutch John, who doesn't particularly enjoy physical contact.

As we deviate further from the main clump of rides and games, sparse trees litter overgrowth along the dirt path that clumsily transitions into gravel.

The funhouse is unassuming from the outside—the entrance a rickety wooden shed covered with fraying splinters of wood. Behind it, colorful circus tents rise, vibrant colors muted by darkness and low branches. An employee with a bored face and splotchy red paint smeared across the tip of his nose leans with his back against the door, holding a cigarette between two fingers and expelling streams of white smoke from his nostrils.

John scrunches his nose at the exhaust. "Maybe Conner's right."

"Hm?"

"The location—the line—is telling. Isn't it?"

Red velvet ropes snake to and fro without a single queuer. We're at the tail end of the fair; only the dark forest stretches after the tents. Other than our apprehensive footsteps crunching closer, and the muffled tinkling of carnival music inside the attraction, the air is quiet.

"It's not a big deal," I say. "It's probably mostly little kids who aren't tall enough for the other stuff that go through here. And it's late, so they're all in bed by now."

The employee's cigarette drips dying embers onto the gravel. He stomps them out. "You need two tickets for the funhouse each."

I tear off two tickets from my sheet to hand over as John does the same. The employee kicks his heel against the door twice and it pops open. A clown with two black, curly pigtails pokes her head out and widens her eyes at us.

John quickly steps behind me. "Aren't you going to explain where the emergency exits are, and any safety protocols?"

The employee shifts the cigarette to the corner of his mouth. "If you get lost, wander around, and you'll find your way out eventually."

I usher John inside as he mutters under his breath. "What an idea."

The door slams shut as we step inside. Red and yellow lights illuminate the narrow hallway we're meant to follow. A hidden, hissing machine ejects thick and musty puffs of artificial fog around us. John swipes his hand through the air and snakes his left pointer finger beside his nose to clear haze from his lenses. "What if we were asthmatics? Do they not take precautions around here anymore?"

The clown from earlier pops her head onto John's shoulder. "Better move it."

He slams his other shoulder against the far wall. "Are there any more of you in the house?"

I loop my arm around John's and pull him down the hall. "You heard her. Better move it."

John shuffles alongside me with his neck craned to watch the clown as she waves goodbye. "Funhouse. This is supposed to be a fun-house. Not a haunted house."

The attraction reeks of disrepair. Sweet, rotting wood hides behind shabby decorations. Plastic-coated clowns giggle from broken speaker boxes that pop and crackle with static.

The first time our father took us to the fair, we were ten years old. John was too scared of the wobbling rides sat upon cinderblocks to try any of them at first, so the only entertainment he sought was the funhouse. While Conner and I sat across from one another and spun in circles until we saw duplicates of each other, our father walked John through the funhouse over and over until they ran out of tickets.

I vaguely recall the visits in the years after that one. New rides and carnival games came and went. Conner and I ran from booth to booth, attraction to attraction, cotton candy sticking to our fingers, our hair frizzing with flyaways. John continued to walk the funhouse up until a few years ago when he resigned to sitting to the side with a greasy paper bag full of popcorn in his lap.

I'd never been to the funhouse in all that time, but I can tell seven years did a number on it. John scrunches his nose at the decor as we pass. "I remember it being...better somehow, but I can't quite figure out which part."

We enter a room full of inflatable clowns stuck to the floor. John clasps his hands together as he shoulders through grimy nylon. "I remember it being a lot cleaner."

The last room is the hall of mirrors, of course. It's not so much a hall, but a maze.

Hundreds of Delilahs and Johns watch as we walk with our hands out to stop ourselves from smashing our faces into some kind of fake glass. Grubby fingerprints smudge the same surfaces from other visitors' explorations through the maze.

The funhouse lights split my face between red and yellow. Somehow, I still look better than I did this morning. The hollow look in my eyes is gone, replaced by...I'm not sure, exactly. Not hope, but acceptance maybe. The girl in the reflection is a changed Delilah. She sees things—she can't control that—but she can deal with it. She's strong enough to do that much.

I move to the next mirror where my body distorts until my head is a balloon about to burst and my legs are popsicle sticks. "Hey, John, come see this one—"

I turn, and John is gone. I scan the mirrors for his duplicates. They're gone too.

The mirrors warp and change, shifting from distorted images of my body to clear, picturesque images of the forest that surrounds the fairgrounds.

Oh no.

The flashing lights fade, replaced by the white glow of a full moon. Fog seeps from the ground to slither from the mirror. Trees grow from the forest floor next. Stiff, bare branches jut out of each weathered frame. The atmosphere turns to ice. My breath fogs in front of my eyes.

Then the mirrors are gone, and I'm standing alone beside the quiet still of the forest late at night.

I look down at my body. Khaki shorts stop right above my knees where long, pale legs follow, ending in beat up sneakers with laces so tightly knotted they're never going to be undone.

I walk alongside an empty road to my left. The dense edge of the forest towers to my right. There are no streetlights to guide my way. No street signs or landmarks I can pinpoint either, but somehow, I know where I'm going.

Fallen leaves crunch underfoot. They are not the bright yellow and faded orange of fall, but blackened. They crumble into a fine dust that blows away in the frigid breeze.

It's winter. I could be seeing—experiencing—something that happened six months ago, or years ago. The body I'm in, the highly-likely-to-be-dead person, shivers and wraps their arms around themselves. Laughter and music echo in the distance and I make my way toward it, shambling like a drunk.

I open my mouth and belt out a song, something popular on the radio last year. My voice wobbles and the lyrics trail off only to pick up again a verse later. The lyrics are also wrong. *Ah, so we are drunk.*

I stumble forward and fall flat on my face on the cold, iced-over asphalt. My knees slide across frozen pebbles, and they imbed in my skin.

I stand on shaking legs. Trickles of blood race with gravity to meet my shoes.

Lights from behind make me turn. The fuzzy shape of a car pulls up beside me. I can't tell if it's black, white, gray, or some other color as my vision is lensed with blurriness.

The window rolls down, and the driver leans across an empty passenger seat to look at me. "Need a ride?" I squint my eyes. I recognize his voice. I don't, but this person does. Yet, they can't place him in their mind. The moonlight fails to reach inside the car to illuminate his face and give any hints either.

"Are you headed to the fair?"

I nod and it makes me so dizzy I lean over and gulp in cold air. His voice means safety. That's the only feeling I can pull from my experience inside this person's body. His voice brings images of warmth, safety, protection, and power. So who is he? A father? A brother? Family of some sort, I assume.

"You don't look good. You should go home. Let me give you a ride home." He does not phrase any of this as a question. He's not family then. Family would mean going home with us, bringing us home—not simply offering a ride.

"My friends are at the fair." My voice isn't nervous, just confused, unfocused. I sway as I stand upright. The laughter and music are still far away, but I can hear them better now. I pick out familiar sounds—the carousel, a miniature rollercoaster with a five-foot drop, several spinning rides painted various neon colors.

I shuffle forward again. The car cruises beside me still, matching my slow pace. "Get in the car."

"No. I'm meeting my friends."

"We've talked about this. Remember? You were caught driving drunk."

"I remember!" The scream shoots up my throat so fast it brings acid with it. I lean over to the side of the road to spit it out. "You're the reason I'm walking in the dark like this!"

"Better than driving. It's for your own safety. I need you to get in the car. Your friends aren't real friends. They're bad news, and you're gonna get hurt."

"You're trying to trick me!" I point at the man hidden by shadows. "You're using me to get to my friends." I drop my arm and stumble. I catch myself on the open window of the passenger door before my knees collide with asphalt.

The man is fast. He shoots from the driver's seat out of the car. He grabs me by my waist and pulls me into the backseat. The drunk goggles don't help me—Delilah me—pick up on any discernable details.

My arms are too weak to fight back with more effort than a light shove that doesn't fully land. Only a few fingers brush against his shoulders.

He clamps the seatbelt across my lap and pulls it taut. The polyester edges dig into my hip bones.

"My friends are gonna be looking for me!" I yell as he slams the door in my face.

When the man gets back into the car, he rolls up both windows. We speed past the fair so quickly the lights blend together in an abstract yellow and blue painting. I hold one hand against my mouth and another on my stomach to push down vomit.

Even in this drunken state, I feel something amiss, a cold dread filling the hollow of my bones as we take winding, dizzying turns deeper into the forest and further from my home.

We pass a marker, indicating we're now five miles outside of town.

"This is the wrong way," I say, turning my head to watch the darkness grow from the back window as the lights of Baneberry Grove disappear around a bend.

The man does not speak. His eyes remain fixed to the road. He doesn't even spare a glance to me in the rearview mirror.

I lean up to him, in between the front seats. "This is the wrong way. I don't live over here." He smells woodsy, like a fresh-cut Christmas tree.

I reach for the lock on the door and try to pull it up. My fingers feel like freshly boiled noodles and are too weak to pry the black stud from its firm hiding place.

"What are you doing? Don't touch that," he says. His voice is stern, and it makes my heart ache. Whoever he is, he doesn't bring this person the feeling of safety and protection anymore. Only fear. Cold and heavy. It pools in my stomach first before running into my fingertips, my toes. The weight of it almost hurts. It's dizzying and sickening, a primal feeling humans were meant to evolve away from hundreds of years ago.

The fear is sobering. The haze of my vision clears slightly. I take note. Short brown hair shorn close to the scalp. A thick, square jaw. Shadows conceal his eyes still, but I now have two more details than before.

Of course, a hairstyle can change. It usually does after a murder. It must help the killer feel safer—harder to catch—to change their appearance.

"Where are we going? Where are you taking me?" I ask. My arms drop to my sides, deflated, as worry replaces bone. A white post shoots past my vision, another five miles distance from home.

He doesn't answer. Of course he doesn't. He continues along the winding roads with a clenched jaw.

I jab the red button on my seatbelt and it flies from my hips to snap against the window and behind my seat.

"Stop—"

I ignore the stranger and throw my body against the door. "Let me out!"

"Stop this!"

"Let me out, now!" I scream. I beat my fists against the window. The glass is sturdy.

"Emily—" the man warns.

Emily! I can't forget that name. I repeat it in my mind—the Delilah mind—even as chaos unfolds in front of my borrowed eyes.

"Let me out!" I screech. I grab the metal buckle and hit it against the window. I only have enough energy to expend four strikes. A small crack forms in the space I pummeled. So small, a sharp stray rock pinging from the bed of a truck could have done the same damage.

He pulls the car over with a squealing hiss of brakes.

I suddenly feel embarrassed, and heat climbs up to my cheeks. I overreacted. I know this man, and I tried to shatter his car window.

The feeling is quickly squashed when he opens the door beside me so violently, the hinges fight to keep the door bolted to the car. He buries his fingers in my hair and tugs me from the backseat.

"Let go of me!" I dig my heels into the dirt and reach behind my head to punch his arms.

My fight doesn't even impede his speed. He is brisk, dragging me from some dirt road I've never known through the brambles at the side.

I try to roll my body out of his grasp, but all I do is hurl my sides into sharp sticks and firm logs, knocking the wind from my lungs.

I claw for a weapon by my side. Only rocks find their way into my hands. They're too small to fight with, comparable to those colorful pebbles strewn along the bottom of a fish tank.

I reach out to prod a stick or branch. One of my fingers bends painfully. A crack tears down the middle of my nail as it burrows within rough bark. I wrap the rest of my hand around the stick as the stranger pulls me to my feet and shoves me backward.

I catch myself before I stumble too far.

I raise my arm above my head. The stick teeters between my fingers.

Three pops ring out before I can bring the branch down on his head.

I stagger until my back presses against something smooth and solid. The branch suddenly feels so heavy it hurts my fingers. I unfurl them, and my weapon falls beside me.

My legs give out next, and I slide down to the forest floor.

The man returns a shining tool from his hands, pointed at me, to hide underneath a button-downed shirt.

His hand shakes as he rubs it against the stubble of his head. He turns and walks through the forest, back the way we came.

Although I wasn't able to fight him, I left an obvious trail in my wake. A person-sized circle cuts through thick underbrush, and a line of dirt has been smoothed over from where he dragged me.

Two car doors close and he drives away.

A gasp of air leaves my lungs and a coughing fit comes with it. I hold my hand up to my mouth. Liquid shoots from between my lips.

I bring my palm into silver light spilling from the space between naked tree branches creating a skeletal web above my head. It's blood. Why am I coughing up blood?

I lean my head against the solid trunk behind me. I gaze up at the sky and recognize the spindly limbs above my head. This is our tree. We come here after school. To smoke, to drink, to talk. To be ourselves without disdainful, watchful eyes on us.

Relief washes over me, replacing the cold of the night. They'll come here after the fair. Or tomorrow after school. Either way, I'm safe here until my friends come for me.

I close my eyes and listen to mother nature's bedtime routine. Owls cry out their goodnights while small critters scurry to beds within tree trunks.

This wouldn't be the first time I've slept under our tree. It's my second home. Close to becoming my first.

My eyelids flutter closed. Exhaustion courses through me, depositing weights in my veins. I feel a tiredness in my bones I've never felt before as the cold night seeps into my chest.

Shallow breathing tears its way through my lungs as my body relaxes.

I'm so tired, I don't even open my eyes as heavy footsteps break free from the overgrowth in front of me.

They walk toward me silently. It must be my friends. They've found me.

Something solid and warm knocks me from the vision and I land on my butt—hard. My jaw clenches down on my tongue, drawing blood in between my teeth.

"I'm sorry, I didn't see you." A figure stands in a corner between mirrors. Lights flash across his body, but only graze the points of his face: upturned nose, rectangular jaw.

"But in my defense," he says, eyes glowing green against black, "who runs headfirst through a hall of mirrors? You could have hit the glass."

John is here now, wrapping an arm around my shoulders to help me up. "Who goes backward in a straightforward funhouse?" he snaps at the stranger yet to step away from shadows.

"The mirrors are tricky; I got turned around."

"Sure," John ushers me in front of him, a palm protectively glued to my back. I don't have time to study the stranger more before John pushes me through the next room and out the exit marked by red and white striped streamers.

"Hey, wait up," the voice calls from the darkness.

"Let's get out of here. We should find Conner."

"I'm fine, really. That guy was right. The mirrors are tricky. I got turned around too, but I'm fine." I look into the trees, the darkness around us, and wonder if Emily's body is still out there somewhere. Did her friends really find her? I hold my body still as shivers race through my limbs.

"Sure you are." John looks back and forth between the hurried steps catching up to us and the rest of the fair up ahead. He grips my forearm and pulls forward.

"I'm not, like, an actual baby. I can walk." I thought of all people John would be the one that wouldn't treat me like some freak made of glass panes held together by duct tape. We always had a special bond—a bond of 'sharing a mutual space without questions, judgment, or talking of any kind.'

"He's bad news."

"Hey, I said wait up!" The stranger catches up quickly. He's...kinda cute, actually. Tall, and muscular but in a way that's not obvious. He could probably bench-press me easily but wouldn't brag about it. He has hair so blonde it could be platinum. One flat mole sits below his left eye and every blink sends his eyelashes down to caress it. Bad news? That can't be possible.

"Delilah, right?" He sticks out a hand following an arm full of prominent veins that rise past the surface of his skin.

I watch John through my peripherals. He scrunches his nose as if he's chasing away a bad itch. It's one of his tics that says he's either irritated or uncomfortable. Conner and I both suffer from the same subconscious giveaway.

I shake the stranger's hand. Bad news to John could mean anything. It could mean the guy talks too much or reads the wrong kinds of books. "That's me. And this is my brother, John."

The stranger smiles; his two front teeth slightly overlap, one pressing in on the other. "I already know John, and Conner—we're on the same wrestling team."

So bad news in this case is the fact that the guy is a wrestler. John detests the sport. He's constantly spouting random facts about the rate of injuries and permanent brain damage to convince Conner to quit and seek a safer hobby. It hasn't worked yet.

The stranger tucks his hands into the front pocket of faded denim jeans. White paint spots run down his right thigh. "I just wanted to say welcome back. I heard you went away for some kind of family function. I'm sure your family missed you."

John rolls his eyes and huffs out a sigh. I flick his arm behind my back. So that's the lie everyone is going with? I was away for family functions. And nobody bothered to ask what family? It's just the four of us, nobody else. I guess strangers wouldn't care to find that out, or have any reason to question it.

"Happy to be back."

"I also want to apologize for knocking you down earlier. I'd say I owe you one, wouldn't you?"

"We don't have time for apologies that take this long," John butts in. He pokes my shoulder blade a few times. I get the hint, but I just got back, and a cute boy wants to offer me a chance to cash in on something that doesn't involve a family terrified to say or do anything around me.

"What do you have in mind?"

John jabs me harder, and I shrug him away.

"I have twelve tickets left and the Ferris wheel is six. I'll treat you to a rather pricey view of town."

"Sounds fun, but I don't like heights." Wow, thirty seconds into a conversation and I've already ruined my chances. *Nice going, Delilah.* I wish I had done anything other than watch my own feet when we walked in and I'd have a counteroffer to make it clear I'm still interested.

"I'll protect you," he offers with another smile and a blink of long, dark lashes. He holds his hand out, not for a shake this time, but with fingers slightly spread apart, inviting me to trust him.

I take the offer.

"Delilah!" John grabs onto my upper arm. "We're needed elsewhere."

"It'll only be a few minutes. We can do the funhouse again after, okay?" This time without a vision to interrupt the experience...I hope.

John's eyes dart from me to the fair again before he takes off running.

The stranger squeezes my hand with calloused fingers. "I'm Dylan, by the way."

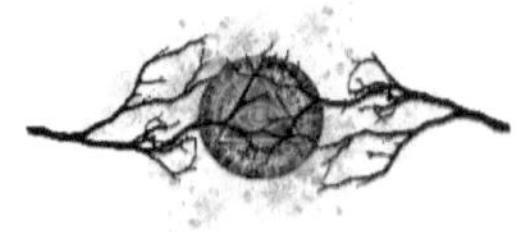

Dylan is true to his word. As the Ferris wheel picks up speed and rattles upward, he stretches one arm around my shoulders. He smells like mint and something sweet I can't place.

I press clammy palms against my thighs. We've been sitting in silence since the bar came down. Dylan admires the view of dark treetops and taps his foot against the air to the tune of tinkling carousel music down below. The silence between us isn't awkward, but I still want to talk. Dylan doesn't know about the incident, where I've been for the past several weeks, or about any of the quirks that put me there. This is a chance for a fresh conversation, a fresh interaction with someone who isn't on standby for my inevitable mental breakdown.

"Can I be honest about something?" Dylan asks.

Relief expands in my lungs. I breathe in the cotton-candy-scented air. "Anything."

"We've actually met before."

The relief is gone. My lungs shrivel up into raisins.

Dylan laughs. "You don't need to look so guilty. It was years ago."

"Are you sure it was me you met?" I wouldn't forget Dylan. Not with that mole. Those eyelashes.

"Wrestling meet when Conner was fresh on the team. You were there with your other brother. I waved to you guys, because I thought you were on the school yearbook team."

I nod as the memory registers. I was investigating a case wherein I thought a parent to a member on the rival team was poisoning wrestlers—fishing for a forfeit. I had been taking pictures of the adults nearest to the water cooler.

I was wrong, by the way. It was someone on the home team doing the poisoning. He wanted to—I don't know—be the top wrestler? Rise in the ranks? The motive didn't make a lot of sense, and he got caught because he didn't wash his hands after dumping rat poison in a cooler of grape-flavored water.

John was there to be Conner's personal water boy, and I was there to make sure I didn't get another vision of a boy throwing up blood until he was comatose.

Dylan looks at me. He blinks slowly, his eyelashes caressing the little mole under his eye. "You didn't wave back."

I whisper an apology. Dylan's smile never falters. "I forgive you, and I'm starting to enjoy messing with you. Your cheeks turn pink, like a sunset."

We reach the peak of the Ferris wheel. My stomach quivers when I lean forward and watch miniature people embark on rides of their own or shop at stalls of greasy foods and absurdly large stuffed animals. Dylan's arm around me tightens, pulling me against his warm, solid side.

Dylan tells me a story about his latest wrestling meet and the opponents he had to face. I nod along as I follow the story, my eyes sweeping from the fair to the surrounding woods and highway back to Baneberry.

I freeze, breath stuck in my throat, as my eyes settle on the shape of a small, circular clearing the opposite way to town. A large tree juts up in the middle, shooting past all the trees in the surrounding forest. I squint and lean forward. It doesn't do anything, but I feel like the movement clears my mind.

I recognize that tree. Bare, gnarled limbs stretch, clawing at the sky. That was the tree I saw in my vision, it has to be. *Emily.* The name warps my insides, creating a pretzel almost as twisted as Conner's favorite snack. That's where the girl from the funhouse died.

"Woah, hey, are you alright?"

I snap my head to the side so fast I have to close my eyes and shake away dizziness. *Don't hurl, Delilah.* That would be embarrassing in front of Dylan, of course. But it would be worse to ruin someone's long, inescapable Ferris wheel ride by covering them in whatever comes out of an empty stomach.

Dylan pulls me closer to him, so close I feel like I'm infiltrating the thin fibers of his t-shirt. The heat of his body is a brand, scarring the skin of my cheeks permanently pink.

"I really don't like heights," I gasp as we finally begin our descent, and my stomach plummets faster than the ride ever will.

"I'd like to check on you later and make sure you made it home alright."

I look into Dylan's eyes, neon like a glow stick. "Alright." The ground comes at us too fast now. I want a few more minutes on this little bench, sitting beside Dylan, pretending nothing else matters. Up here, the air is cool, pristine. I'm safe from a vision, from brothers that don't know what to say around me, from our father's questioning looks.

"Can I get your number? I need to make sure you don't have any nightmares after this and that I made a good impression." When he winks, it sends my heart fluttering like a bug trapped in a jar.

I recite my number and wonder if my phone can even accept calls and texts from unknown sources. Our father might have found a way to block that too.

Dylan flashes me a smile and a wave after our feet meet the ground again.

I rejoin my family, hovering around another food stand. Conner beams at an employee as he orders various flavors of ice cream in cups for all of us to try. Nobody mentions Dylan or questions the way John nervously scrunches his nose.

G ood morning, mademoiselle," Conner says. I shut my eyes a second after opening them when he tosses my curtains to the side, letting in the blinding orange glow of a sunrise. "Your presence has been requested downstairs."

I sit up in bed and scowl in his direction, my eyes squinting slits.

Conner holds his hands up in surrender. "It is not I, m'lady. The man of the house wishes to speak with you."

"Did I hit my head in my sleep?"

"Maybe? Or my impressions are so good you believe you've been transported into another time. One with jousting tournaments, backstabbing royalty, and an absurd amount of nudity."

I rub sleep from my eyes. I tossed and turned most of the night. Images of the deaths of two girls took turns in the spotlight. "What time is it?"

"Almost seven." Conner exercises in place, lifting his knees to his chest and down again. "About to go on a jog. Wanna come? I'll wait for you."

I shake my head and yawn. I'll be going back to bed after this mysterious meeting our father has called. He hasn't spoken to me one-on-one like this since before I left.

Conner continues his stretching steps down the stairs. I shuffle behind him, both hands clinging to the support of the banister.

John is already awake, pristinely dressed, and headed to the kitchen. Since when did my brothers get up so early? Summers are for sleeping in and staying up late. At least, they were four weeks ago.

Our father's office door is open. He sits behind his desk, dressed as nicely as John. He raises his head when I shuffle into the doorway. "Good morning, Delilah. Would you like to sit down?"

"No, thank you." I've never stepped foot in his office before. None of us have. This is the first invitation he's extended to his children. The space has always been for clients.

Even though he's invited me in to take a seat, I don't think I could. Invisible lasers would cut my body into abnormal cubes and filaments. Or an alarm would blare. Red lights would blaze. A team of men with guns and dressed in black would take me away.

Our father waits a moment. He doesn't seem to mind his very first invitation ended in rejection. Instead, he stands to meet me at the doorway. "John informed me of last night. You met Dylan Walker?"

"Yes." It's unlike John to tattle. My brothers and I tend to keep our issues and disagreements between the three of us. We've never struggled to work something out. We always come to a consensus or a compromise, eventually.

"Do not spend anymore time with him."

I blink up at our father. Why does he care? Better yet, *when* did he start to care about me?

"I understand you feel you've found a new friend, but I assure you, Dylan Walker is not a friend you want. He is a client. You cannot see him anymore."

"What did he do?"

Our father sighs.

"Well, how long will he be a client for?"

"That's not the point." Our father breathes in deeply through his nose. I wonder if he does this during trials, when the witness on the stand doesn't give him the response he's looking for. What is he like outside of my world? Is he secretly kind, loving, empathetic? Does everyone else get to see something my brothers and I don't?

"Delilah, do you understand what I'm telling you? No contact with Dylan Walker."

"I'm not dumb. I understand." The frustrated words sting my lips as they pass. This is our life now, isn't it? At odds, suspicious and malcontent, with each other because of what happened.

Our father returns to his desk. He sits at a computer and taps away, signaling our conversation is over.

I return to my room, under warm blankets, and stare at the ceiling.

Dylan is a client. That's why John considered him bad news. But John can't possibly know what Dylan—presumably—did to need our father as a defense attorney. Our father would never give away that information, and my brother would never snoop through files or listen in on appointments.

Whatever Dylan did or did not do can't be that bad. Vandalism? He doesn't look like a vandal. Loitering or trespassing? This is a small town. People are protective of their private land. Maybe he found himself at the wrong place, an inch into a stickler's property.

All my thoughts of Dylan must have found their way to him, a thrill in his stomach or a flutter in his heart. My phone pings as a message from an unknown number pops up:

Sleep well?

-D

Maybe it's a wrestler thing, and Dylan doesn't sleep in either. That wouldn't explain John's early start to the day, but nothing could. John is John, and that's that.

I bring my phone closer to my face.

I'd love to take you out today. If you're not already sick of me.

-D

I'm not concerned with Dylan's potential wrongdoings. He can tell me if he wants, or he can keep it a secret. I'm not one to judge. I've witnessed two murders since my return, and I'm not doing anything with that information. If anything, I'm the biggest transgressor in Baneberry—maybe in the world.

I type out a quick message to Dylan. Something about him is magnetic. I don't want to be in this house, lifeless and cold, with a family afraid of me—for me.

I want an escape. I want someone who talks about fun things without watching me from the corner of his eyes—searching for a sign or symptom that doesn't exist.

And maybe a small part of me, hidden in the recesses of my mind and heart, wants our father to keep caring about what I do.

Dylan arrives as the sun dips behind the trees. I hear his motorcycle before I see it. The motor whines and screams. The sound bounces off the trees before he reaches the incline to the house.

I hover by the front door, waiting to slip out once he gets closer.

The noise draws my brothers.

Conner looks out the window, a frown growing on his face. "Is that Dylan Walker?"

John, halfway down the stairs, with a book near his nose, closes it with a thud. He stampedes down the steps to join Conner at the window. "Yes it is, but he doesn't have an appointment."

No use in being sneaky now. "He's here for me," I say.

"You can't see him, Lilah," Conner says, his eyes frozen wide. "He's a client."

"He's under investigation," John adds. "He's dangerous."

"I'm sorry, Lilah, I really am," Conner says, "But I need to issue a veto for this decision."

"I second that," John says, his hand raised in pledge.

"You can't veto who I talk to." Veto is a word my brothers and I use when we heavily disagree with something. John raised veto when Conner tried to enter some sort of truck smashing competition. Conner and I both raised veto when John mentioned an interest in late-night birdwatching by himself deep in the forest. Veto is undeniable—under normal circumstances. No one has ever raised it against a date, a meeting with another person for any reason. Veto is for actions, not interactions.

Dylan rings the doorbell. My brothers talk over each other. Each spouts the same rendition that going out with Dylan is a bad idea and I need to stay here.

"You shouldn't be talking to him. His—"

I slip out the door and close it on John's words.

Dylan wears a black leather jacket and has a helmet tucked under his arm. "They sound excited."

He hands me a spare helmet with a heart sticker peeling off the side. Red fades to pink from plenty of time in the sun.

I've never ridden a motorcycle before. Dylan is patient as he instructs me on how to balance my weight and where to place my feet.

He slips the helmet over my head with a smile before donning his own.

"Hold on tight," he says as the engine wakes with a roar.

My stomach quivers as we race down winding roads to the heart of Baneberry. I clasp my hands together along Dylan's abdomen as I rest my covered cheek against his back. The leather jacket warms my torso, and through the wind, I pick up the faint smell of wood smoke.

Despite the precarious start, maybe I have figured out how to be new Delilah. As warm, sun-soaked air whips across my body and billows my t-shirt, I finally grasp the meaning of what it is to be carefree.

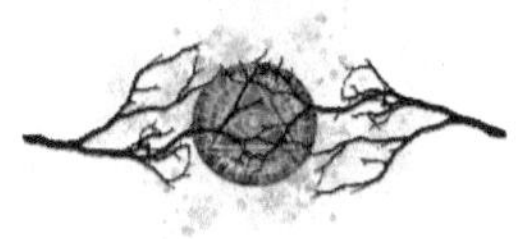

We take seats outside the ice cream parlor, a banana split in white ceramic between us. Dylan places a glob of strawberry in his mouth with a little red spoon. "So...your brothers didn't seem happy to see us together. What kind of reputation do I hold in your house?"

Jitters run up and down my whole body from the exhilarating ride over. My skin feels different, barely attached, and a little weightless from the lack of rushing wind. I feel as if I am the air itself, hovering atop the ground. "All I know is you're one of our father's clients." I use my own little red spoon to scoop up a sample of chocolate ice cream. "Whether that makes you a thief, a fraud, or a murderer depends on what you tell me."

Dylan smiles lopsidedly as he bites down on a cherry and flicks the stem into a pot filled with an assortment of colorful flowers beside our table. "How kind of them to let me paint myself in a pretty light."

"So which is it?" I tease.

"My girlfriend is missing."

"Oh." I lower a spoonful of whipped cream topped with sprinkles as my stomach drops. Bloody images of mutilated bodies in the forest and the hulking figure that stalks them flash across my mind.

"She has been for a few months now. Since before you left actually. Investigators seem to think she's not coming back. That *I* had something to do with it."

"You're saying you didn't?" I drop my tiny spoon back into the bowl. The boys were right. I shouldn't be seeing Dylan. This was a mistake. I can't get involved—I don't want to. That's not who I am anymore.

Dylan's gaze drifts to the rainbow of flowers. They seem to droop as his eyes fill with tears. "Of course I didn't. I loved her."

I stand and brush a stray yellow sprinkle from my jeans. Thankfully, home isn't too far from here, even if I have to walk. I can always call Conner to pick me up. Though, that might end in an 'I told you so.' "I'm sure your lawyer has already informed you not to refer to lost or missing loved ones in the past tense. It makes you look guilty."

Dylan grabs the hem of my t-shirt as I turn away. "Please stay. Let me explain. I want to tell you my side."

I hesitate. The charm, and good looks, and smile aren't new. I've seen it from dozens of bad people committing bad acts. It doesn't mean he's innocent. But, our father is the one defending him. He wanted me to stay away so I wouldn't impede on an investigation, I'm sure. If Dylan was responsible, our father would have made his warnings clearer, urgent. Far more direct.

I'm not naïve enough to believe our father never defended a "guilty" client. However, the man has the occasional flair up of morals. He wouldn't support someone outright evil. He wouldn't defend a boy that murdered his own girlfriend.

Dylan releases my shirt and smoothes out the hem. "Five minutes? It's all I need. I'll even let you have the rest of this. No more sharing with a potential criminal."

I sit with crossed legs and arms. "Your time starts now."

Dylan pushes the rest of the banana split to me. The chocolate scoop is half-eaten and melting along the bottom. Half a glob of strawberry leans against it. The vanilla scoop and both slices of banana are untouched.

"Brit—she's a fighter," he says. "She's a wrestler like me. It's how we met. During a scrimmage before the boys and girls' teams went to our first tournament." He inhales deeply through his nose and twists a thick, gold ring around the middle finger of his right hand. "I believe Brit left of her own accord. I don't think she's missing, like, in danger *missing*. I think she chose to leave."

"Wouldn't your girlfriend tell you if she was planning on leaving town?" I poke the melting ice cream with my spoon. Girlfriend. He has a girlfriend. I can't believe he took me on the Ferris wheel, on the motorcycle ride, out for ice cream when he's had a girlfriend this whole time.

"We weren't too close before she left, or disappeared, or whatever you wanna call it. We had practice, tournaments, college applications, finals...we were busy. Hence the past tense reference earlier. I'm not even sure she *was* my girlfriend by the time she left. We hadn't spoken in two weeks."

I split the strawberry ball in half and scoop up a mouthful. "Why are police and detectives investigating you then? Why do you need a defense attorney?"

"Her parents insist she had no reason to leave, and I'll admit they make a good argument. She has good grades, good scholarship opportunities. She loves her family, her friends, her town. But she disappeared. No trace, no note, no nothing. My dad hired your dad to defend me because the police said I did something and hid it. But I didn't, I swear. I wanna find out what happened to Brit as much as the others. I want to make sure she's okay."

I save the chocolate scoop for last. A cherry burrows halfway down the dollop, only its stem poking up. I fish it out with the spoon and extend it to Dylan. I don't like cherries. Or sunflower seeds. Or anything that has me sorting through the good and the bad of food as it sits on my tongue. "Are you investigating? Are you planning to find out what happened to her?"

"I was actually hoping you'd be able to help me with that." Dylan smiles again. It turns my stomach. Not because he has a bad smile—it's the opposite. It's warm and inviting. It makes me want to smile back, even if this isn't a conversation where that facial expression is necessary. I can't fall for the smile. The long, batting eyelashes. The sympathy and pity. I'm done. I have to be done. If I help Dylan, I have to help the next person who comes along. Then the next after that. It will never end. I have to be the one to make it end.

"You could have told me what you needed from the start." My emotions are a rollercoaster. No—a wreck. Jagged, steaming steel and spattered blood across windows. They can't settle on any one feeling since my return.

Dylan drops the cherry on the table and grabs my hands. He rubs his thumb along my knuckles. The gesture stills the flow of blood throughout my body. "I'm not trying to waste your time or mislead you. I'm not sure what it is about you. Maybe it's your quick mind, or some kind of intuition, but I know you've helped your dad on some odd cases—helped him catch terrible people. I thought that if I gave you all the information I have, you'd help me. You'd help us clear my name."

Delilah, don't you dare fall for it. I don't do this anymore. I can't. I vowed to stay out of investigations. I was sick. I went away. I got better. *I'm better now.*

I can't drag myself back down. Not for anyone. Not even the boy with the lopsided smile, the rough yet soothing hands, and the genuine innocence. The word *no* sits on my tongue. It begs me to reconsider. I wish I could swallow that word and give Dylan what he needs. I wish I could help, I really do. But I can't. It's too dangerous. If I give any more of myself to the dead, I won't have anything left. I'll be a shell, an empty husk. A shed skin.

I slip my hands from his to tuck them against my lap. In this moment, the decision feels like the hardest I've ever made. "I'm sorry—I really am—but I don't help with those kinds of things anymore."

Dylan nods once, a frown tugging his lips. "I understand. Thank you for taking the time to listen."

"I'm sure the truth will come to light, with or without my help. The detectives in this town are good at what they do."

It's not a lie, but it's not the whole truth either. The detectives generally end up in the right direction. Sometimes they need a nudge from our father about client privilege confidentiality and the hints his clients are willing to offer. The hints are really from me, but they get the murders and disappearances solved nonetheless.

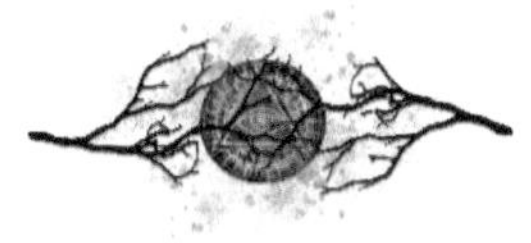

The ride back isn't nearly as thrilling. Dylan doesn't treat me any differently after my rejection, but I feel like a disappointment. I barely wrap my arms around him as we take the same winding roads home. I blink back tears before removing my helmet and returning it.

Dylan walks me up to my front porch. Yellow bulbs of fireflies light our way as crickets sing.

Inside the front entrance, I notice my father's office door is closed, but the blue glow of a computer screen seeps under the door. Classical music plays somewhere upstairs, likely in John's room as he studies, or reads, or does whatever it is John does behind closed doors. Sports commentators cheer and yell in Conner's room. The boys are all occupied. They've already moved on from my return.

"Hey, just so we're clear," Dylan says, leaning through the door frame, both hands gripping the top, "I wasn't using you. This really was a date. And I had a really nice time."

"Do you want to stay a little longer? We can hang out. Talk?" I still wish to revive whatever this is between us. Dylan's girlfriend is missing, and I've refused to help him find her. He has every reason to say no. To vow to never see or speak to me again. But, I've enjoyed our time together. The way he talks to me about life and wrestling and other topics so easily. He isn't afraid to say the wrong thing. He doesn't think he can damage me further, unlike my family.

Dylan drops his arms by his sides and sticks his head through the doorway. "I would hate to turn down that offer. Are you sure it's okay?"

I dismiss his concern with a wave of my hand. "They won't even notice. Everyone treats me like I've got the plague around here."

Dylan closes the front door behind him and secures the lock. "Should I be worried about catching something from you?"

I turn to the stairs to hide burning cheeks. Terrible wording. The plague? Seriously?

Dylan stands beside me, his shoulder playfully bumping into mine. "I'm kidding. I know that's not what you meant."

An electric shock travels up my veins and shocks my heart when Dylan takes my hand. He follows me up the stairs onto the second floor.

The only place to sit in my bedroom is on the bed. The sheets are crumpled from this morning. I quickly adjust them to lay flat across the mattress. We sit side by side, our backs pressed against the wall.

"Can I ask you a personal question?" Dylan asks.

I shrug. "Sure."

He plucks a loose thread from the bedspread and pulls it taut between his pointer fingers. "Why do you call your dad 'father?' I thought that term was outdated. You only hear old-fashioned, rich people in movies say it." He chuckles to himself quietly.

I nod. It's a fair question. Sometimes I forget other families aren't like mine. Other kids have dads. Papas. Not fathers they're unwilling to claim as their own.

"It just seems unnecessarily fancy," Dylan adds. "I thought maybe he preferred it since he's this local celebrity lawyer figure. Maybe Dad is too bland and informal for him."

Dad is a strong word. One with meaning and positive connotation. Nathaniel Dufort is not a dad. He is nothing more than a father. A word I would prefer to use—if it was an acceptable title—would be DNA-sharer. A bill payer, perhaps. A man that lives in the same house as me. That might be the best title.

"We all call him father, our father, because that's how he introduced himself to us. 'Good morning, Conner, Delilah, and John. I'm your father.'"

Dylan laughs. It's contagious and forces me to smile. His laugh makes me think of a breeze on a hot August day—refreshing. "He introduced himself like that to babies?"

I shake my head and let out a small laugh too. "No, we weren't babies when we met him. We were eight."

"You didn't meet your dad until you were eight?" Dylan lifts one of his knees up to his chest and lays his head down on it. He looks at me with big, soft eyes. It makes my heart beat faster, and a herd of butterflies nest in my stomach. "Tell me everything you can about yourself, Delilah. I want to know you."

Nobody has ever wanted to know me before. Nobody has ever cared for what I had to say, except my brothers, and maybe our father when he's fishing for a vision. I am the unsocial one. The unapproachable one. The weird girl who is always stuck at home sick, missing weeks of school at a time, because my visions can be crippling. Even John has more friends than me, and he hates talking to people.

I copy Dylan's pose. Our faces are so close together, our noses nearly kiss. "Well, my name is Delilah. I have two brothers. Our father is a lawyer. And I just got home from a trip."

Dylan laughs again, and it sounds so sweet I want to stuff it in my ears like cotton swabs.

"What about a mom? Sorry, a mother?" he asks with a smile.

I scrunch up my nose. "Long, long story with a not-so-happy ending."

Dylan lifts his head up. "I get it. It's like that for me too. No mom, and my dad—well, he's a real piece of work. Might just rival yours. Distant. Strict. Harsh." He holds up his fingers, ticking off each description.

"Ours isn't all that strict. Or harsh. Distant, though. He is that."

Dylan blinks in what I think may be understanding. His eyes focus on a corner of the room, but his gaze is far away.

"My brothers and I," I continue, speaking a truth aloud more for myself than for Dylan. "We always felt like this…pothole…sitting on the road of our father's life. His tires got stuck one day, and he's been there ever since."

Dylan looks at me now. His eyes are clear. He's seeing through me—seeing me. Understanding me in a way I've always wanted to be understood by a person I didn't share blood and a birthday with. My brothers and I commiserate with each other, but it's different with Dylan. He doesn't really know what it's like because he isn't here. And at the same time, he knows what it's like. He's living a similar life with a similar father somewhere else.

"He stays not because he wants to, or because he particularly likes this life with us, but out of obligation." I speak a truth I've known in the back of my mind since I was eight and our father rescued us from a life of drifting after our mother's death. It's a truth I've known for years, but it still stings to say it aloud. To give the words a space to evolve and take up thoughts in another's mind. I'm admitting to Dylan something I have a hard time admitting to myself—I am unwanted.

Dylan brings a hand to my cheek, his thumb resting on my chin. "We're the same, Delilah."

He leans in to kiss me.

As his soft lips press against mine, all thoughts of Brit's disappearance and the visions I've had since my return are gone.

A small fraction of me, a miniscule dot in the back of my mind, wants me to feel guilty. I'm kissing another girl's boyfriend. It doesn't matter that they were on rocky soil, or that Dylan might as well be single because they drifted far apart before she went missing. But a bigger part of me, the ninety-ninth percentile of my brain tells me this is okay. She didn't want him anymore. He can be mine now. I can comfort him. I can rebuild him.

Dylan and I fall back together, sinking into bedsheets. They envelop us, cool and soft. Dylan's lips are like fire as they scorch a trail from behind my ear to my neck. My breath catches in my throat, and I have to remind myself to breathe. Don't be a freak. Don't ruin this. Enjoy it—see what happens. See what we can become together.

His lips trace along my jawline. My stomach flutters with each flap of butterfly wings. I squeeze my eyes shut.

Dylan shifts his weight. His knees dig into my hips. He grips my wrists tightly, pinning my arms to my sides. I open my eyes.

Dylan is no longer here.

Now, it is some man I've never seen before in my life.

The soft sheets beneath me are gone. Instead, dry sticks and pointed pebbles dig into my back as I thrash and fight him off of me.

"Stop squirming, little girl," he says. Several of his teeth are missing, while others are rotting out of his mouth.

I free one of my arms and bring it up to his face, jabbing my fingers in the indented spaces under his eyes.

He grunts and hits me across the face. My head falls to the side. Tender skin scrapes against old, wooden floorboards.

A chorus of screams sound just outside the wooden double doors behind him. Other girls, perhaps? Girls like me, who have found themselves in a terrible place with no idea how to get out?

He grabs my face, thick dirty fingers digging into the bruise forming on my cheek. He turns my head until I look at him again.

"You know why you're here, girlie?" I—Delilah—note his features. Hair covers up any identifying attributes along his jaw and chin. It's a dark gray, not yet fully changed by age. Layers of grime cover tanned skin from a lifetime of working in the sun. His eyes are strikingly blue—eyes you'd find on a model, a pilot, someone of noteworthy importance. His nose is wide and flat, traveling nearly the same width of his face as the beard.

He brings his knee up to press into my stomach. A groan slips from my lips. "Did he tell you why you're here? Did he?"

I can't breathe. Can't talk. Can barely even think. I shake my head.

"You've been bad. Bad girls come to me. I know what to do with them."

He reaches for a grungy, dull blade with metal teeth on the floor beside him. I throw my head back and scream.

Pressure lessens, releasing my arms from my sides, and I set them against a solid chest and push back hard. Dylan is here now, and he stumbles off of me and slips from the bed.

"What happened?" he shouts, not in anger, but surprise.

I bring my legs up to my chest and hold myself there as shudders take over my body.

"I think you should leave." It's the easiest solution. I can't explain what happened, not to someone I only recently met. And I can't face him. I can't look into his eyes, as striking as the strangers.

He kneels at the side of the bed, his hands clasped together as if praying for my forgiveness. "Did I do something wrong?"

"You need to leave." I hide my face as unshed tears turn my cheeks pinker than the earlier blush that was once there.

"Delilah," he whispers, "I'm sorry for whatever I did wrong. Please let me fix this."

"Get out, Dylan! Leave!" My shoulders shake as the tears break through the brittle wall I've built myself.

Dylan hesitates only a moment longer before slinking from the room.

I fall back onto the bed again and stare up at the plain white ceiling above me.

Why do I try? Nothing will ever change. I can't ride a bus without a vision. I can't visit a fair with my brothers. I can't kiss a boy.

I practice the calming exercises I learned over the last several weeks. I breathe deeply, close my eyes and count to ten. I pinch myself to stay grounded.

This is my body. I'm in it. This is me, not someone else's tragic reality.

Even as the tears cease and my breathing evens, my brain spins around the same question. What is the point? Those girls died. Even if I didn't see—experience—the final breath, I know they didn't make it out of those situations alive. There's nothing I can do about it now. The bad things have already happened. So what's the point of me?

I sit on the shower floor as the water turns from hot to warm, then warm to cold, then cold to frigid. A pool of icy water builds in my lap and around my thighs as I sit cross-legged. Goosebumps prick my skin and my teeth chatter, but I can't move. I can't burn or freeze away that feeling. Strong, rough, scarred hands gripping my wrists, holding me down with a force that liquifies my stomach. I can't clear the smell of his breath from my nostrils, meaty, like he chewed on a jerky stick. I can't forget the fear that held me down along with him. That filled my bones with lead. That overflowed from my stomach to my throat and choked me.

I only stand when Conner bangs against the door with a closed fist, shouting that he and his sweaty gym clothes are stinking up the hallway, and if I didn't hurry, the smell would penetrate my closed bedroom door and stain my fresh linens.

By the time I exit the bathroom with a towel wrapped around my shivering body, Dylan's motorcycle is gone and dinner is on the table in the form of a grocery store rotisserie chicken and freshly baked sweet rolls.

In bed, I cry myself to sleep. Then again the next night. And the night after.

I've seen all kinds of horrific injuries. A gunshot to the head that gave me a migraine for a week. Falling down the stairs and breaking several bones in my body, including my back—I could only sleep on my left side after that one. I was even strangled at one point. Pale, veiny hands wrapped around my neck. A fingernail nicked my chin. I broke out of that vision with a sore throat and a missing voice. I was ten, and a nurse called CPS during a routine checkup after noticing several bruises along my arms and legs from a myriad of other nightmares I witnessed weekly.

But this was different. I've never felt so powerless. Afraid. I have to wrap a rubber band around my wrist and flick it every time my mind drifts and imagines what might have happened to that poor girl next. The part I didn't have to see. Torture? Dismemberment?

I think I would prefer a gunshot to the head over what I had seen. Or strangling, or drowning. Even all three at once. Anything other than being held down, confined so intimately.

It's unfair. Everyone else gets to live a life they want—to an extent. But I'm stuck in the tragedies of others. And as much as I hate it, as much as I wish, pray even, that I could be free of these visions forever, I can't sit on them and do nothing. Whoever hurt that girl, or the one beneath the tree, or the one running, screaming, and pleading in the woods—I would find them, I would catch them, and I would make them pay.

I find Conner in his room, flipping through magazines with some kind of competitive wrestling match on the TV above his dresser. He lifts his head and pulls out an inviting smile. "Hey, Lilah. What's the haps?"

"I don't know what that means, but I need a ride."

"Perfect! I need some fresh air." He flips off the TV and bounces from the room.

John pokes his head in the doorway. "I want to go on a ride."

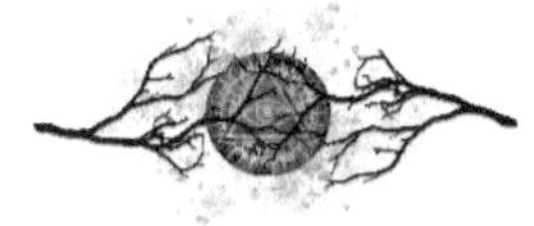

The three of us make our way down a desolate highway. Conner sings along to whatever is playing on the radio these days while John presses his forehead against the warm glass window and watches trees and bushes fly past.

I scan the side of the road and tree line in case a lost, half-dead girl wanders out in the road for help. Not that she would. She's been dead for several months by now—maybe even years.

When we reach the stretch of road I believe may be the one I'm looking for, shortly after a 10-mile marker, I tap Conner's shoulder. "Pull over here, please."

He complies with confused brows. "What for?"

I unlock my door. "I'll be right back."

I hop out as John and Conner look at each other and back to me.

My estimation is surprisingly accurate for such little information to go off of. I find a makeshift dirt trail that cuts through prickly green bushes and yellow wildflowers. It leads to a clearing.

Patches of dirt take up most of the space, only broken apart by tramped down grass. Discarded glass bottles nestle in brush, flowers, against the trunks of trees. There's even a small campfire pit dug by hand. Jagged rocks create a ring around the edge, but there's hardly any ashes left in the pit. This tells me a few things. This is—or was—a popular hangout spot, but nobody has been here in a while. Long enough for the ashes to blow away or soak into the dirt.

I walk around the clearing, picking up loose pieces of trash to search for any meaning behind them. The bottle labels are faded from the sun. How long would that take? John would know.

A tree stands as a monument in the center of the clearing. It's taller than the squat pines around it. It's also bizarrely bare. Not a single leaf clings to the branches or settles below. Several naked arms project in all directions. Roots emerge from the ground, curved and ever-diving, like little, brown Loch Ness Monsters.

I crouch down to study the place where the girl may have fallen. I lean back against the tree and look up. It's what she saw. The only difference is the sky. Her night versus my day.

A twig snaps from where I came, and I lift my head.

John and Conner emerge from the path together.

Conner points a finger at the tree and smiles. "Hey, an octo-tree."

John studies the bulky branches down to the trunk where I sit. "You made us wait in the car so you could visit a tree with eight roots?" He stands still, hands on his thighs to lift his slacks just above his ankles.

Conner joins me, sighing as he leans against the trunk. "Does this place mean something to you?"

I turn around, crouching again, to study the rough bark by dragging my fingers across it. "Not to me, no." My fingers brush cold metal and I tip forward. The blunt edge of a bullet sticks out of the wood. I hook my fingers around it and pull. It doesn't move.

"Do you have tweezers in your truck?"

Conner leans in beside me. "Is that a bullet?"

"Yes, and I need it. Do you have something to get it out?"

"Why do you need a tree bullet, Lilah?"

I sigh and look at him. He wouldn't understand. Neither of them would. Conner isn't dumb, and neither is John. They'll figure it out, eventually. But for now, I'd rather not bring up my visions. I'd rather keep them silent from our father, who would eventually hear about it through one of them. "Do we really have to talk about it? I just need it, okay?"

Conner looks around and picks up a rock with a sharp tip. He begins to carve the bark around the bullet. I stand and let him work. John still hasn't moved. He scans the tree line like a guard on duty.

I circle the tree. No blood. No body, obviously. The body would have been removed. She would have been taken to a second—no, a third—location. Or else whoever hung out here and made that fire pit would have reported her to the cops the second they saw her. But who's to say this wasn't reported? And what if this girl is Dylan's Brit? I rub tiredness from my eyes. This will be exhausting—investigating alone.

"Aha, got it!" Conner says, holding the bullet above his head triumphantly. He hands it to me, and I turn it over in my palm. I've never seen a bullet before. I'm not sure what I expected. Not a name, of course, but at least a measurement, or a serial number of what store it was bought at.

John joins us, scrutinizing the small metal pellet. "Is that a bullet?"

"It was in octo-tree," Conner says.

John looks at me, his eyebrows down-turned. "Why are you pulling bullets from trees, Delilah?"

I sigh again. "This is why I wanted you to wait in the car. It's not important."

"It is important," he protests. "What crime is this linked to?"

Before I have to explain myself, Conner answers, "I don't think this is linked to a crime, or else we'd have heard about it. Probably from people playing target practice," he gestures to the bottles around us.

"Those bottles aren't broken. Not a single one," John says.

I slide past them and back to the road. I've found all I could here. It's time to talk to Dylan again. The timeline doesn't make any sense, but I still want to make sure it wasn't Brit I felt die underneath that tree.

In the morning, I find Conner doing those knee-lifts in the kitchen. Dylan hasn't answered the pathetic apology I texted him last night. I can't tell if he's mad at me, or if he's blocked me. The next best option is a face-to-face conversation.

"Hey, so, um, I was wondering if I could tag along," I say, holding my hands together behind my back.

Conner drops both feet to the floor. "To practice?"

"Yeah. I want to go to the gym, do some laps, maybe watch you throw some guys around."

Conner shakes his head and tucks a handful of granola and cereal bars into the pockets of his gym shorts. "Why? You aren't even dressed for it."

I look down at my black pajama shorts with little red hearts and my oversized white t-shirt. These could probably pass as workout clothes to someone really far away with bad vision. "I haven't had a chance to stretch my legs and get some exercise since I left, you know? I just think I could really benefit from it...mentally."

Adding the mentally at the end seems to be the catalyst that gets me what I want, because Conner tosses me a protein bar and gives me a ten-minute countdown to change into something appropriate for public wear.

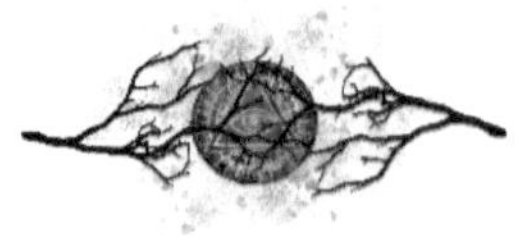

I find Dylan once his practice finishes. He's alone, gulping down water from a fountain beside the locker room.

He's either a weight lower or higher than my brother, but I don't remember or care to remember which. I'm just glad they're not the same so I can talk to him alone.

He wipes sweat from his brow and throws a white towel over his shoulder when he sees me approaching. Droplets glisten along his shoulders to drip down thick, veiny arms. "What are you doing here?" His tone is without anger or annoyance, but guarded. Like I might be someone else in a Delilah disguise. I don't blame him after my meltdown a few nights ago. If I was in his non-slip black sandals, I'd probably just ignore me.

"I came to apologize, and to explain."

Dylan reaches into a black duffel beside his feet to pull out a plain white t-shirt. "No need to explain. I took things too far, and I'm sorry."

"You really didn't. I liked what happened between us."

The muscles of Dylan's abdomen ripple as he lifts his arms over his head and trades his damp tank top for the clean shirt.

"You said you knew I helped our father with some of his cases, remember? You guessed one reason was my intuition. You were right. I feel things, see things—things that can't always be explained."

Dylan zips up his duffle bag and throws it behind his back, the strap drawn across his chest. "What kinds of things?" He doesn't even raise his eyebrows or the pitch of his voice at the end of the question. He doesn't care. He's acting nice. Making polite conversation because of the minimal history we share.

I look around the room, cautious of peering eyes and listening ears. Everyone else is on the other end of the gym, lounging on bleachers or fighting on blue mats. The person who attacked all the girls I've been seeing lately could be listening. I lean into Dylan. Even after his workout, he smells like a combination of mint and freshly cut grass. "People. Places. Murders."

Dylan's eyes grow and his face pales. He leads me by my upper arm into a corner hidden between two stands of mini bleachers. "You're playing with me, right?"

I lock eyes with Dylan. "No. I see those things. I see them nearly every day. Different events, different people, but always something bad. Something tragic. Something that's already happened, and I can't stop. I can only deal with the aftermath."

Dylan shuffles his fingers across the top of his head, puffing up his once neatly combed hair. "I'm sure you do your best."

I had opened my mouth, ready to defend myself, but close it in surprise. Dylan is the first person to know about my visions outside my family. I had expected—I don't know—maybe more questions. More prodding as to why I couldn't help. I had expected someone to speak to me the way I speak to myself—full of disappointment and blame. I choke out a quiet response. "Thank you. I do."

Dylan leans away, pink returning to his cheeks. "That kind of information can change lives. How do you even 'deal with the aftermath?' You tell the police and they go catch the bad guy?"

Our father always instructed me not to tell anybody about the things I saw. Other than him and my brothers, he warned, nobody could be entrusted with what I've witnessed. It could be used against me. Or I could be hurt if someone who committed a malicious act wanted me to keep quiet.

Dylan is the first person I've trusted enough to confide in. I'm not entirely sure why. Maybe because he's like me. Misunderstood by his father, and searching for answers he'll most likely never find. He certainly wasn't a figure in my vision, unless he's found a way to shrink since then. He isn't a killer—he won't kill me. "The police won't listen if I walk up and say 'I saw a murder in my mind,'" I explain. "Our father usually handles that part. I tell him what I see, and he deals with it. I don't know what his process is, but he's never failed."

"Why are you telling me this?" Dylan makes sure no one else is listening when he leans in close; his lips graze my ear and ignite a flutter in my stomach. "Did you see Brit?"

"No. Well...I don't know. I hope not. What I saw was awful, and I sincerely hope it wasn't Brit. But then that means it was another girl."

Dylan watches me patiently, almost eagerly. I'm sure it's hard to hear this, to hear the person you care about might be—but also might not be—the person I've seen murdered. He's stuck in a limbo between closure and uncertainty. A terrible impasse. He either has to hope I see a vision to know what happened to Brit, but then she's likely dead. Or hope I don't see a vision. Then Brit could be alive, but also could be dead, and now we can't find out who did it. There is no happy ending here.

"I'm telling you this because I'm sorry for how I acted that night. I had a vision, it was bad, and I panicked. I wasn't freaking out because of you. We just had very poor timing."

"You saw another murder?"

"Not quite. I saw the part before the murder. I know that poor girl didn't make it out of there alive, but I can't tell you exactly how she died. Or if it was just after the vision, or if she was tortured first."

Dylan's face falls. "Oh. And you're sure it wasn't Brit?"

I'm not sure Brit wasn't the one who suffered that fate. But whoever she was, I won't let her disappear at the hands of that man. I'll find out what happened. I'll do what I can to bring her justice.

"If I ever were to see Brit," I say, "I wouldn't know it. I don't even know what she looks like."

Dylan slings his duffle bag on the floor and drops to one knee to search through it. He hands me a picture from a polaroid camera. The edges of the photo curl inwards from constant movement alongside sweaty clothes and deodorant sticks.

In the square center, Dylan has one arm wrapped around the shoulder of a girl with blazing red hair cut in a bob that stops at her chin. Her skin is darker than his, inky and beautiful. I grip the aging corners of the photo. The white rectangle on the bottom has the words *Brit and Dyl* in thin cursive writing.

"She's beautiful," I say.

Dylan smiles. When he looks at the photograph, his eyes are soft. He must be optimistic. I would look at a photograph in despair if my loved one was missing. "We took this in September. She got the camera for her birthday and made her mom take the first picture with it."

"It sounds like she's loved."

"She is." Dylan gently takes the photo from my fingers. He tries to smooth the curled edges before setting it atop his other belongings and zipping the bag up again.

My name echoes around the gym. Conner is looking for me. I turn with a plan to sneak out and reveal myself without Dylan in tow, but Dylan catches my elbow. "Wait—so who did you see? Was it Brit?"

"Not Brit."

The relief is a ripple through Dylan's entire body and his fingers go limp, dropping my arm.

I should warn him—this isn't necessarily good news. It's mediocre at best. Just because I watched some other girl die doesn't mean Brit is alive and well.

My brother finds us before I can tell Dylan not to hope too much.

"What's going on here?" Conner asks, arms crossed.

Dylan picks his duffle bag off the floor. "We were just catching up. I'm heading out now." He says goodbye to me in the form of a shy smile. I return it.

When I look back, Conner is watching me. His face is unreadable, as if he's channeling John. *Great, lecture incoming.*

Conner closes the front door carefully with a soft click. He's trying to handle the situation as if I'm some scared, wounded animal or feral child. "I don't wanna use the whole 'I'm the oldest and you have to obey me' argument."

"Then don't." The ride home had been silent and tense. Conner probably practiced this speech in his head the whole time, planning to walk the line perfectly in between strict and amiable. The cool brother I can talk to—so full of wisdom and guidance. But to me, his opener sounds too much like a spy for our father trying not to give himself away.

Conner raises his voice and follows close behind as I stalk into the kitchen. "Dad specifically asked you not to have any association with Dylan."

"So he's Dad now?"

John lifts his head hovering over a bowl of blue and pink fruits mixed in with creamy yogurt.

I open the fridge and pull out a carton of orange juice. "He asks us *all* not to do things that we still end up doing."

"Yeah, well, this is different. That guy is dangerous. You shouldn't be around him anymore. Especially not alone."

"Wrestling is dangerous. Mountain biking is dangerous. Laying underneath your huge, heavy truck to work on it is dangerous. You don't see me trying to stop you."

John chimes in, "He's always been Dad, Delilah. We just didn't see it until recently."

"Since when?" I throw my free hand up. "You couldn't stand the man a year ago. What's changed?"

"He has," Conner says. "He's not like you remember. You need to give him a chance like we did. He cares now. He checks on us, he does nice things for us. He knows what's best for us."

"You're picking *his* side over mine?" I slam the carton on the granite countertop. Droplets of orange splash against white and gray stone.

Conner steps to me, holding his hands up like I'm a wild stallion he's about to get kicked in the face by. If the intent is to calm me, it's having the opposite effect. I want to hurl the carton at him. They're all acting like I'm crazy. Like I can't be trusted. Like I belong back in those locked white rooms.

"There are no sides," Conner says.

John stands to deposit his empty breakfast bowl into the kitchen sink. "Yes, there are. I am on Dad's."

Conner shakes his head. "Don't you remember our talk on sensitivity and empathy? Kid gloves," he adds with a whisper.

"I'm not a kid!"

"No, you're not, so you can hear this." John places both hands on my shoulders and turns me to face him. He's shorter, but only by an inch or two. Most people we meet think Conner is older by a year and John and I are twins. We're both on the shorter side, around the mid five foot mark. We're both scrawny, and gangly, with pale skin and dark hair and eyes. The complete opposite of Conner's sandy hair, tanned skin, sparkling blue eyes, and bulky, towering frame.

"Delilah, you're my sister and I love you, but you were out of control. I am on Dad's side," John says.

I shrug his hands off my shoulders. So much for us against him. A motto we've kept for years. A support system we held onto even when we fought, even when only one of us was in trouble with our father. It was always the three of us against him, against the rest of the world. He was the outsider to our triangle. An extra point we didn't need. A member far too late to the party.

"I don't know if I would use the words 'out of control,'" Conner interjects.

"I would. You were a mess, Delilah. You were dangerous, raving, and I'm not convinced that's completely in the past," John says.

"Okay, I think that's enough." Conner pulls out his cellphone and pelts the screen with quick finger taps.

"You're gonna get him involved now? After what he did? He sent me away. Forced me to leave. He abandoned me."

"You tried to kill yourself, Delilah! You tried to leave us!" John drops the typical expressionless look he wears daily. His voice wobbles and his eyes glisten.

"And the answer to that is to separate me from the people I need most? It was vicious retaliation for ruining his pristine image. He's no longer the do-it-all successful lawyer and single dad the rest of the town saw, right?" My whole body trembles as I yell, my voice drowning out the noise around—the buzz of electricity coursing through the refrigerator, water pelting dishes currently being sanitized in the dishwasher. White spots impede my vision as my heart beats in my ears, in my brain. "I embarrassed him, and he needed to get back at me."

John shakes his head as I talk.

"Why don't we sit down and discuss this calmly," Conner says. He's always the mediator of me and John's outbursts. He gets it from our father.

"You were sick! Nobody knew what to do! Dad didn't want to send you away, but it was the only option." John's voice cracks on the word sick, like it's a painful thing to say.

"Stop covering for him!" It's like the world got flipped upside down after I left. I didn't expect to come home to perfection, but at least some semblance of normalcy. I didn't expect my brothers, my two closest confidants, to gang up on me. To blame me for what happened. To believe him—believe that I needed to be sent away.

"It's true," Conner says. "You can be mad, but you can't blame only Dad. We all agreed on what to do."

"Why didn't anyone ask what I wanted?" I slump in a chair and rest my head on the walnut wood tabletop. I feel my entire family is against me. Plotting my path and forcing me down it. I was the one banished from our home, but somehow I'm the bad guy. I'm the one who made the mistake.

My brothers sit on either side of me. "Do you know why we didn't visit you in the hospital?" Conner asks. "Dad didn't want us to see you like that. He said it wasn't fair to anyone, including you, but he gave us the rundown. It wasn't good. I mean, how much do you really remember?"

The therapist in the mental care home thought I had 'dissociative amnesia following acute trauma' because I wouldn't talk about that night. But I do remember it. I was tired, exhausted. The horrible visions, the unsolved cases, the knowledge that anywhere I went, traumatic memories of another person could assault me became too much. The pressure to solve every wrongdoing in town drained me. The guilt when I was too slow or missed a crucial clue, numbed me into nothing. It was too much. I didn't want that life anymore. I wanted to be done. Finished with everything. Free. I've changed my mind since then. But it doesn't seem to matter. They're still stuck on that event.

John's leg bounces up and down in quick succession. "He said you were delirious. You kept asking him to let you die."

"I've accepted my abilities," I say as I sit up. "Or at least, I've accepted there's nothing I can do about them. They won't go away—they're who I am."

"You're still having visions?" Conner says. He and John both exchange a look. One that I used to share with them whenever someone said something odd and we knew we would discuss it later.

I gesture to the ratty hair secured into two french braids on my head. Plenty of strands stick out and float in the breeze of the cool AC. My shirt is wrinkly and I've worn it since I got out of the frigid shower several days ago. "Why else would I resemble a walking corpse? This is the 'I'm having horrible visions again look.'"

Conner taps on his phone screen again. Skipping emojis to go straight for detailed sentences.

I steal the phone from his hand. "Stop tattling to him. I'm telling you this in confidence."

As I suspected, Conner and our father have a string of messages about me.

How's your sister doing?

Does she seem okay?

Make sure she doesn't investigate.

Is she still having visions?

Conner snatches the phone back to tuck in his gym pockets. "We all thought they were gone. He's just checking on you."

"I'm fine, okay. Can we all forget about the last several months and go back to normal? Please?"

John and Conner exchange their look again.

"Stop looking at each other! Let's just move on and pretend nothing ever happened."

We sit at the table together, silently. They might not forget, but at least they stopped talking about the incident for now.

John breaks the silence first, which is odd because John never chooses to start a conversation. "So what did you see about Dylan and his missing girlfriend?"

"Nothing. He didn't do anything to her."

"And you know that because?"

"Because I've seen different girls attacked by the same guy, maybe even two different guys, but neither of them are Dylan."

"And you know *that* because?"

"Because, John, Dylan isn't a creepy lumberjack bashing girls' heads in at various locations."

"Clarify."

Conner elbows John lightly, a reminder to mind his manners. Or he's still stuck in the mindset of treating me with kid gloves. I'm glad John has dropped it, or maybe he never possessed the ability to act that way in the first place. I need somebody around here to treat me like I'm still the Delilah they know and care about.

"Please," Conner adds.

"Unless Dylan has been sneaking around hurting different girls in different places throughout the entire year or so—while wearing some pretty in-depth disguises—he's not the one we're looking for."

"Looking for? Who said anything about looking for?" Conner stands and paces back and forth. He snaps his fingers silently as he thinks. Another one of our shared tics.

"Yeah, I thought you were done." John stares at me, our chocolate-brown eyes arguing through our lack of words.

"So you both think I should just sit around and do nothing? Shake off the visions and what? Not help."

"Yes."

"Kinda."

"Well, I can't. I thought I could, but I can't." I hold myself as a shiver runs up my spine. A knot forms in my throat, bringing stinging tears to the corners of my eyes. I shake the memory of the latest vision from my head. I've been chosen somehow. Forced to bear the burden of some sort of extra sight. Who would I be if I saw what I saw and did nothing? I can't ignore the dead's last moments—their cries for help, for closure from the grave.

John continues to bounce his leg up and down under the table while Conner presses his lips together. "So where do we start?"

"What do you mean?" Conner can't be saying what I think he's saying. This is my awful battle, my burden to bear. I'd never dragged him into my cases before, and I won't be starting now.

"What's the first clue?" John adds.

"I don't really have any clues yet. The visions aren't like they were before. Or maybe I'm not like I was before."

"I didn't evolve to possess the ability of mind reading while you were gone," John says with his signature flat expression, "so if you could start explaining things more thoroughly..."

"John," Conner warns.

I smile and bark out a laugh. I've missed this more than I realized. "So, how it used to work was I'd see them less randomly, well, kinda randomly. I was more in control, though. For example, if I walked by the site of a murder, sometimes it would trigger a vision of the actual murder. But I could also interact with objects or other people who had known, spoken to, or even just passed by the victim. I could step into their shoes however I wanted and see whatever I needed to see."

"And now?" John doesn't look at me. He studies the natural grooves in the wooden table as he traces them with his fingertips. I can always tell when he's ignoring me or not by the way he tilts his head towards me, signaling that he's listening. Meanwhile, Conner studies me like a hawk, eyes barely blinking, as though the action will bat away the words coming from my mouth before they reach his ears.

"Now..." I send a whoosh of air from my lips. "Now it's not as often and not as controlled. Every time I've had a vision has never been when I wanted to, and I can't quite figure out what triggered them. Plus, when I touched a picture of Dylan and Brit together, nothing came up. I feel..." Lost? Confused? Like my visions are controlling me instead of me controlling them. "...blocked, I guess."

"What could have caused that?" Conner slowly retrieves his phone from his pocket. I glare at him, and he pushes it back into the fabric.

"Medications is the only answer," John says. He slaps the table and stands. "I'm going to do some research."

"Research on what?" Conner and I say at the same time.

"On our first lead, clearly."

Ralph's Pit Stop is the first lead John finds from his research. By research, I mean he opened a web browser, typed "Baneberry Grove map," and found the closest destination between the two places that may have triggered my visions—the bus stop, and the fair. The third place, my bedroom, is something I've left out of the discussion for now. I'm not ready to talk about that one. I've already wracked my brain to figure out the trigger and came up blank. For now, it's a vision best left to the side.

Ralph's isn't much of a lead, I know, but we don't know where else to start. The clearing with octo-tree didn't yield many clues, and wandering aimlessly through the forest in the hopes of another vision sounds like a waste of time more than anything else. Plus, Ralph's is on the very outskirts of town, so any of the girls could have stopped, or passed, by there before they died.

Conner drives, gripping the steering wheel so tight I'm afraid the bones hidden underneath the skin of his knuckles might burst out into the open air. John sits in the backseat with thick black headphones plastered to his skull. A hint of classical music trills from them.

That leaves me to take up the spacious passenger seat. I snap my fingers silently in my lap as we pass rows of dense, clustered pine trees that block out the sun along the two-lane highway. Sun, snow, and thick tires have worn down the yellow paint that separates the two lanes. A thin streak is only visible between every three to four lines.

"Did you tell *him* where we're going? What we're doing?" I ask.

Conner flicks his eyes to the side to look at me and loosens his grip slightly, bones retreating into his hands. "No."

"But you want to?"

"Does it matter?"

Yes. It does, but ultimately it's my decision to keep our father out of this. "I don't want to make you lie to him."

"Believe me, I'm not. I won't."

"Oh yeah, I almost forgot. After I left, you became his number one fan. His closest confidant. His right-hand—"

"It's not like that, okay," Conner interrupts. "He's changed a lot since you left. He's gotten better at showing that he cares about us. At listening. At being a dad instead of just a father."

"So I'm the one who held him back?" I whisper.

"That's not what he said and you know it," John says from the backseat. He pauses the classical music, but keeps the headphones on. The only background noise now is the rumble of the truck engine.

"I'm sure you feel a little left out, being gone for four weeks," Conner says, flipping the left blinker and turning into a wide road with four pothole-scarred lanes instead of two. "You came back and everything is different, and Dad is different, and we get along now."

I nod. I feel more than a little left out. A lot left out. Like I left my family behind and came home to aliens wearing Conner, John, and our father as suits.

"We were worried about you and became unified in this fear. It strengthened us, I guess. I think it made us appreciate each other," Conner thinks aloud, slowing the truck onto crunching gravel as Ralph's Pit Stop grows near.

John lowers his headphones to rest behind his neck and leans forward to stick his head in between the two front seats. "Great. We saw it, and it looks horrible. Let's go home and tell the police to check this place out."

"We just got here and have exactly zero leads to give over to the police," I say. "Believe me, we'll need a lot. They don't run on hunches like in TV shows. At least not in Baneberry."

"At least one percent of long distance truckers, the ones that go across the country coast to coast, are in prison right now for serial murders," John says matter-of-factly, pointing to the row of eight semis parked at the edge of the gravel lot.

"Only one percent? I thought it would be more," I say.

Conner shakes his head as he shifts the truck into park. "That's ridiculous. One percent? It would probably be the same amount for any profession then. One percent of truckers, one percent of mailmen, one percent of teachers."

"Yeah, that's a good point," I add. "How many long distance truckers are there? Because if there are, say, seven thousand—"

"It doesn't matter," John snaps. "One percent is too high of a percentage for any of us to go in there. They could be murdering someone right now and we'd be killed for witnessing it."

Conner presses his lips together and looks at me expectantly. John has scared the leadership instinct out of him with his statistics. And he's not used to this, neither of them are. Investigating random missing and-or dead girls by asking probing questions in suspicious places can humble even the most confident people.

I run clammy palms down the length of my twin braids, smoothing floating, frizzy pieces of hair. "You guys can stay here. I'll scream if I need backup."

Gravel shifts and slides under the soles of my slip-on, strappy sandals. Two doors close behind me with loud thuds. A small smile pinches my cheeks as two sets of footprints crunch on the gravel behind me.

Ralph's Pit Stop appears run down and barely functioning. At least, from an outsider's perspective. I can't imagine any customers spending precious free time here, let alone eight. Glass double doors mark the entrance to the building, but only one window is visible. The other has a sheet of heavily graffitied wood plugging the hole where missing glass should be. A pile of swept-aside, shattered shards glitter from the mid-morning sun.

Conner steps in front of us to open the door and enter first. John rushes in too close behind me. The narrow tips of his Oxfords graze the back of my ankles as we huddle together in the doorway.

The door shudders to a close behind us.

I blink erratically to adjust to the dark and dungy pit stop. One man sleeps with his head pressed atop a bar glowing with the sticky residue of spilled drinks. A few patrons crowd around a pool table tucked into the back corner.

John grips one of my arms tight as a blood pressure cuff to keep me steady. Conner takes in every person in the room and picks the one he seems to trust the most to give us information. He leads us to a gap in between two empty stools at the bar. A chalkboard menu takes up the back wall. Grubby hands erased most of the listed food and drink items.

The bartender looks up at the three of us and sighs. "Don't show me no fake IDs. I know you ain't of the drinkin' age."

"We're not here to drink, sir," Conner says.

The bartender leans back in shock. "Sir? Not a single sir in this joint."

"Uh." Conner looks at me quizzically. I shrug. John grips my arm tighter.

"I'm sorry," Conner says. "I didn't mean to offend you. We're here to ask some questions."

"Ain't no ency-clo-pedias 'round here neither."

Conner ignores that last statement and continues. "We're hoping someone around here saw something, or even knows something, about a crime."

The already still bar goes silent. I would have thought we were on a TV show and a viewer pressed the mute button.

Every head turns to stare at us. Even the sleeping patron raises his head and turns. A sticky brown film coats one of his cheeks.

The bartender leans forward, his hand resting in a pool of spilled liquid on the counter. "Now I know you didn't barge in here and ask for snitches."

Conner waves his hands. "No, no, no. Not like that. We're not with the police."

The sleeping patron slides from his stool to saunter up to us. "Who said anything about the police?"

Conner sighs and drops his hands. "I'm sorry, this is getting twisted. Maybe my sister can explain better."

His blue eyes meet mine and I nod.

"We're looking for our friend," I say, glancing from the bartender to each patron, meeting their distrustful eyes. "She's missing, and we think she may have passed by here at one point. She would be our age and look out of place."

The bartender lifts his head, looking at me down his nose. "What's that supposed to mean?"

"It means exactly what I said. Our friend is missing. She might have been here. Did anyone see her?"

John grips my arm so tight I'm shocked his fingers don't punch through my skin to wrap around my very bones.

Conner's eyes flash me a warning to watch my tone.

I don't have all the details, not of the most recent girls I've seen. I was in their bodies, looking through their eyes. The only description I have to offer is of the first girl I saw, running and screaming through the trees. "Yellow and brown flannel shirt," I say as I plant my palms on the countertop, somehow both sticky and gritty, and lean into the bartender's space. "Brown hair." I close my eyes, picture her face, tear-stained and covered in bruises. "She wore leather boots." Blood coated her teeth. Her feet were scratched and torn—from running or from torture, I don't know.

I open my eyes. The sleeping patron sneers as the bartender shakes his head, pretending to clean something. "We don't mess with those girls," he whispers.

"What?" Ice snakes its way down my spine, blocking out the feeling of John's incessant grip. "What girls?"

The patron scoots in beside me and an empty stool. The foul rank of too many drinks wafts from his mouth when he opens it. "Nobody around here knows nothing."

I ignore him, face the bartender instead. He still doesn't raise his head to look at me. "If you know something, you have to tell us. You have to help them."

"I dunno who you think yer talking to, little girl." The once sleeping patron spits brown gunk onto the floor and presses it into the grimy carpet with his boots. Did I see those boots before? Did I see this man's face? If anyone here was a killer, it would be the guy that has a problem with questions.

Conner steps in between us, blocking the man's face from my view. "My sister's just worried about her friend. She's been missing for a while and we thought maybe someone here saw her and could point us in the right direction."

Another man steps up, a pool cue slung over his shoulder. His broad shoulders brush against the first's. He pulls a cap branded with some college sports team low, half hiding puffy eyelids and bloodshot eyes. A tangled beard covers the rest of his face. Brown with flecks of gray. "Naw, you thought you'd come in here spewing accusations. Easier to blame strangers than think maybe the tramp ran off on her own."

"Wow, okay. There's no need for words like that." Conner holds up his hands in his 'taming the wild stallion' pose. It didn't work on me so there's no chance it will work on these guys. "We've asked our questions and got our answers. None of you saw her. We'll get out of your hair now."

John presses his forehead to my back and whispers to himself. "This was a bad idea. Bad idea. Bad idea. Bad idea. Bad idea."

The first man walks in a semicircle to stand behind John, stopping us from our slow retreat while the second stands chest to chest with Conner. "You can't come in here, insinuate, and then walk away just like that. It ain't nice." He peers around Conner's rigid frame to look at me. "It ain't ladylike."

I crane my neck to study the first man. His eyes are blue, but his frame is different. Lean, wiry. A body made up of pure muscle. Stubble covers his chin. His hair is shorn close to the scalp like the man in the car, but his voice is different. It doesn't hold the same power. This man doesn't feel in charge; he's only pretending.

The first man jumps forward and seizes John by the collar of his white button down. John flails around, failing to shake his attacker off.

"Let him go," I scream. Instinct takes over. I've seen too many visions of bad things to not react instantly. To fight or not to fight doesn't always matter. Some people die even after fighting tooth and nail to stay alive. But I won't go down without a fight. Not when John is on the line and has done nothing wrong.

I punch the man's arm, and when he only laughs at the weak force of the blow, I burrow my teeth into his hand.

"What the—"

Conner intercepts with a wrestling move. He wraps his arms around the man's torso and charges forward with his body bent into the attacker's waist. They both go down, crushing a table and its surrounding four chairs.

John clutches me. "Help! Somebody help us!"

Angry hat man steps in, hauling Conner from his position pinning sleeping guy on the floor. He throws Conner back against the wall and delivers a quick blow to his face. Conner staggers. Another blow comes, for his stomach this time. He doubles over.

I take a running jump and wrap my arms and legs around hat man's back. I link my arms around his throat and throw my body backwards—something I've learned from a vision in the past. It slowed down a victim's attacker just enough for them to run a few blocks before being gunned down in an alley.

The man runs backward. He slams me into the edge of the bar. The thick, wooden counter smashes against my spine. I grit my teeth and let go, sliding down until I collapse on the sticky floor.

"Enough. ENOUGH!" The bartender shouts. A shotgun sits in his hands, pointed at the ceiling.

I use the bar to claw my way to a stand as the two men straighten and brush off their clothes. John trembles in the corner by the door, too loyal to run for safety without his siblings in tow.

"Get out. You're banned."

The two men snicker as I loop an arm around Conner and walk him to meet with John.

"You too, Bear, Mitchell. Get the hell out."

John sidles under Conner's other side and runs, nearly tripping us out the door.

I slide too hard on the gravel and lose one of my sandals. John doesn't let me stop; he rushes us to the truck, looking behind him the whole way. "Can you drive?"

"Yes, I can drive," Conner says.

"Are you sure? If not, I can..."

"I'm not letting you take the wheel, Mr. Toad," Conner laughs.

The lone working door of Ralph's Pit Stop opens with a slam against the peeling white siding of the building. I whip my head around to watch sharp cracks explode across the glass pane. The two men storm from the building and break into a sprint towards us.

John and I drop Conner at the driver side door. He jams his keys into the truck and hops in. John and I scramble to throw ourselves into the backseat bench, our legs tangled in a pretzel as we slam the door closed.

"Go, Go, Go!" John yells. Tires spin in the gravel. "Do you want us to die, Conner? Do you!"

"Dude, stop. You're freaking me out." Conner shifts the gears of the truck back and forth and we lurch forward. We fly from the parking lot as the first man reaches the truck and sends out a useless kick that only touches the dust we leave behind.

Tires squeal as Conner jerks the wheel into a sharp turn onto the main road. He winces as he lets out a gasping breath. His eyes find mine in the rearview mirror. "Time to get Dad involved?"

I click my seatbelt into place as I work on restoring my own regular breathing patterns. "Never."

What did I say? Does anybody remember what I said? No? Then I will repeat myself," John says as he pulls a bag of frozen peas from the fridge. He wraps a lime green dishtowel around the bag and bends it to break the frozen pellets up from one big chunk. "One percent. One percent of truckers are in prison for serial murders. And what do you do? Hm?"

John holds wrapped peas against Conner's splotchy, swelling face.

"Do you remember? Because I do," John adds. He retrieves another bag of frozen food, a berry mix this time, and wraps it in a matching lime green towel. He hands that one to me to hold against my aching back. "You antagonized them, and then you attacked them."

"We were defending you," Conner says. He winces and presses the ice pack firmly against his face.

"I give you permission to let me die in the future." John opens the freezer once more to pull out a prepackaged ice cream cone. "Save yourselves. Don't worry about me."

"We would never do that," I say. Our time at Ralph's Pit Stop got bad fast, and it makes me sick to my stomach. Pent up anger and frustration lashes in my mind, and the target is myself. I put my brothers in danger. Reckless, stupid danger. All for a cause that doesn't concern them, doesn't really concern me.

Why do I even care so much? I have nothing to go off of other than the girls' faces. No full names, no ages. I can barely muster up a description of them in their last moments. Or their attacker.

Conner places a hand on my shoulder. "You doing okay?"

I sigh. "Look, you guys, I'm sorry. Thank you for trying."

With a mouth full of frozen chocolate and crumbles of peanut, John tilts his head. "I said let me die, not dump me from your mission."

"I appreciate all you did, but I think it's best if I leave you out of this."

"I think what Delilah means is: let's take a breather, regroup, and try again tomorrow," Conner says.

"Yeah, that's not at all what I mean." I toss my thawing berries on the counter. "I mean, good try, nothing personal, but no thanks."

"Who died and made you emperor?" John fiddles with his ice cream wrapper and stares at the floor.

Conner and I look at each other and back at John.

"An emperor rules over a land or a country while kings and queens only have their small kingdom," John sighs, never missing a moment to educate us, and show off his vast knowledge. "The point is: your rule isn't law. You can't tell me what to do."

"People died! Which is why I don't want you involved anymore. I don't need to add my brothers to the tally."

"How many of these investigations have you done with Dad?"

I tick off check marks in my head of years of cases. I give up after I remember the twentieth one. "Too many to count."

"You're still alive. So is he. That tells me you don't have to worry about us."

"We never started a bar fight during our investigations," I point out.

John tosses his wrapper in the trash. "We live and we learn."

"Considering how bad things could have gotten," Conner interjects, "Ralph's wasn't *that* bad."

"I think you should look in a mirror," I say.

John claps his hands together to gather our attention. "Let's debrief. What did we learn?"

I sigh and rest my forehead against the cool granite countertop. Nothing. I learned nothing. The minimal glimpses of the man, or men, killing the girls aren't enough to know if I'm looking at him with my own eyes. If anything, any of those bar patrons could fit his description. Tall, burly, crude...angry.

"The guy in your visions had a beard, right?" Conner says. "Both the guys that went after us had beards, in a way. And they seemed to take our questions way too personal. That's a red flag to me."

John slips a little spiral notebook from his button-downed shirt pocket and uncaps a pen tucked beside it. "Beard. Okay, what else?"

Conner does all the work I should be doing and gives John other details to add to his list. By the time he runs out if ideas, we have a decent description in one column and the bar patrons with similarities in another column. The only problem is, nearly everyone we saw is in the suspect column.

John reads the list of traits back to me.

When I don't respond or lift my head, Conner pats me on the back. "I know it's overwhelming, Lilah. But the bright side is we have a dozen suspects now instead of zero. That's progress. At least we know where to look."

I raise my head. "Look where exactly? We don't have any names, any addresses, any occupations, any motives. We have nothing other than a list of shady dudes that all look the same, with the same personality. Any of them could have done it. Hell, they could have all taken turns killing someone different."

"Then we'll catch them all, okay?" Conner's voice is gentle and calm. It makes me want to cry. Both of them are being too nice, trying too hard. This mission is a failure. I'm a failure. I can't solve anything. I've never been able to. It was always our father that did the hard part, the thinking part. I've only ever been a messenger. An in between of clues and answers. I'm nothing more than a middleman—a crappy one at that.

John flips the notebook to a clean page. "You've mentioned there could be more than one killer. Why is that?"

"He had a beard—in one of my visions." I snap my fingers in my lap. It's time, isn't it? To come clean about the vision I had with Dylan. If I'm going to accept help, I need to give up all the information I have.

"Which one?"

The words are stuck in my throat. It was close, personal. Transitioning from Dylan's hands to the killer's, Dylan's sweet smell to a rotting, meaty one. I bite back nausea. "With Dylan—in my bedroom."

Conner's arm snaps back to his side. "You brought Dylan here?"

"Delilah," John sighs.

"Yeah, yeah. He's a suspect, I got that. We were just talking, and then..."

"Then what?" Conner asks. John squints at me, a glare glossing over his eyes.

"Then I...kissed him, and..."

"Delilah!"

"Lilah!"

"Then I had a vision and that was it." My fingers still in my lap.

My brothers stare at me. Conner opens his mouth first, "Wait. Does that mean—did you have a vision of kissing the killer?"

"No, no, nothing like that." A shudder claims my spine at the thought. "He was holding a girl down, taunting her. He pulled a weapon out, a knife I think, and it ended."

Conner stands still, rigid, beside me while John pens more notes to paper.

There. All I know is out in the open for them to dissect. Maybe they'll see a connection I don't. Maybe they'll say there's only one killer, and this will all feel a little less daunting. I steer our discussion away from Dylan and back to the killer's appearance. "In my vision with the girl under the tree, Emily—the one I kidnapped beforehand—I don't think he had a beard."

"He could have shaved," Conner says, bringing a tense hand up to massage his smooth chin.

John nods in agreement. "Was there anything else?"

"I didn't get a good look at him the second time. It was too dark." I straighten my back with a grimace as a growing bruise stretches across tender skin. "He didn't talk the same, though. He was more formal.

Commanding. Completely different dialect, actually..." Now that I notice that detail, the answer feels embarrassingly obvious.

In both visions, the men had similar builds. They appeared tall and strong, but they had to be different. Unless one killer was putting on a show, mimicking a drawl among victims. But that wouldn't make any sense. It seems the intention was to kill from the start with all the girls. It didn't matter what they saw or heard if they wouldn't be able to tell anyone.

There has to be two different men—two different killers. If the stomach was capable of flatlining like a heart, that's what mine would be doing. I've never gone up against two killers. Two dangerous men with unknown motives and victims that are all too similar to me—to Brit.

Another clue comes to me, an ache in my head similar to the one across my back. "Did you hear what the bartender said?"

My brothers shake their heads.

"He said 'we don't mess with those girls.' What do you think that means?"

Conner sucks in a breath while John notes my words.

"I believe we found an accomplice," John says, bringing the end of the pen to rest in the corner of his mouth.

"He said they 'don't mess with.' Isn't that, like, the opposite of an accomplice?" Conner asks.

"No, Conner, *we're* the opposite of an accomplice, because we're actually trying to solve this mystery," John says. "They are cowards who apparently know something and stay silent."

My mind swivels between two words. Who is *we*? The men in Ralph's from staff to customer? The three men we interacted with specifically? And what deems the girls I've seen, *those girls*? What is the connection? That's got to be our next focus if we're going to figure out anything.

"Lilah," Conner says, interrupting my brain before it can overheat. "He said we—that's a plural. This is bigger than us. We need to bring Dad in."

"No—never." My brothers both stare at me, as if that will magically make me change my mind, overcome my betrayal. "At least, not right now."

"If that's the case," John says with a sigh, "Conner and I will find out what we can about Bear and Mitchell."

"I'll tackle the victims." There is no conviction in my words. I feel strangely distant, like my mind is floating away from a body glued to the kitchen floor. This is all starting to feel like too much, but if I'm going to investigate my visions, I need to do it on my own terms. I cannot bring our father in here to direct, demand, point at a potential clue and tell me to jump.

Conner's right, though. This is bigger than us. We need backup. And I know just who to recruit.

Despite my brothers' apprehension, I invite Dylan over to assist us the next day. We're going up against two killers, and possible accomplices, with a rapidly building pile of unidentified victims. We need all the help we can get.

Dylan arrives swiftly, rumbling up the drive as the sun breaks over treetops. His timing is impressive—he appears five minutes after our father leaves for work.

He enters the house with a black backpack tucked under his arm. "Can we use your dad's office for some privacy?" Dylan turns the handle of the door.

My hand reaches out quicker than my mouth can respond. It settles on top of Dylan's, holding him from breaching the room. "He doesn't allow anyone in his office. We can use the kitchen; nobody'll bother us."

Our father doesn't have many rules. He has plenty of expectations, but his only true rule is no one enters his office. The only time an invitation has been extended was to me a few days ago—a ruse intended to lower my guard, I assume. If my brothers and I need our father, not that we ever do, we hover around the vicinity until he finally closes his computer for the day, locks up his files, and steps from the room. He's made it clear time and time again: his career takes precedence over everything else.

Early morning sunlight floods the kitchen, stamping slanted squares across the floor. Rays bathe the table in golden light while cicadas hum and buzz in the trees outside. I watch through the large bay window beside the table as a Magpie flits to and from the ground to a tree branch that extends above the second floor of the house.

I pop open the back door to let the summer breeze sweep through the kitchen. The yellow azaleas that grow underneath the window above the sink perfume the air with a muted floral scent. They don't grow here naturally—Conner planted them one year for a science project. We expected them to die, but they flourished instead, and invaded the yard and surrounding tree line.

Dylan upends his backpack over the table. Loose paper printouts and newspaper clippings fall into an unorganized pile.

"I did some research," Dylan says, "after you texted me yesterday." He drops his backpack to the floor and falls into a chair. His hands quickly arrange the papers into random groupings, pages overlapping at the very edges to take up less space.

Missing person's flyers, one record of an Amber Alert for an eight-year-old, an unidentified body found washed up in a river a few towns over. The dates range from six months ago to nine years ago. "You did research," I say.

"If I'm being honest, it was kinda thrilling. I felt like a detective in a movie. I went to the library to print out stuff about missing girls in the area, took a few of these posters from the grocery store's local news board."

I grab the missing poster closest to me. "These girls are missing. Presumed dead."

Dylan bows his head. "You're right, I'm sorry."

The girl in this poster can't be any older than me. A halo of tight braids surround her head. She has a radiant smile that makes her brown cheeks glow. A small gap takes up space in between the top of her front teeth. Twine loosely wraps around her neck, looped around an orange bottle cap that rests against her clavicle.

"She looks like Brit," Dylan says.

According to the short, blocky handwritten sentences that run along the bottom of the poster, she's seventeen like me. Or she was seventeen when she went missing and had this picture taken. She was last seen wearing a beige cardigan over a black tank top and denim jeans with a rip in the left knee. Her last known whereabouts were alongside her friends, smoking behind the bleachers at school. Her highschool is a rival of ours. It's a town over, twenty-five minutes by car, fifty by school bus for an away game.

"Do you think that's important? That she looks like Brit?"

I shake my head, set the poster down, and pick up the one beside it. Another seventeen-year-old girl—from the same school. Her hair is blonde and frizzy like she brushed out tight curls right before this picture was taken, or went over a week without brushing straight hair. Three gold piercings stick out of her eyebrows. Her face looks bored as her gray eyes watch something in the distance.

"She went missing two days before the other one," Dylan says.

I carefully set the poster down beside the first. "Are they all from the same town?"

"No. Just those two. These three—" Dylan passes me a stack of papers "—were from around here."

Four years ago. Five years. Eleven. "These can't be related. They're way too old."

"You think what you saw happened recently?"

"All my visions are from recent events. No older than a year or two."

Dylan tilts his head as he looks at me.

"What?" My hand immediately shoots to my face, my hair, to make sure I didn't suddenly turn into a mess the second Dylan showed up. I brushed my hair today, re-braided it.

Dylan smiles, but it's tinted with sadness and worry as we leaf through the papers. "You're really impressive, Delilah. The way you can pick up on those details."

"Oh. Thank you." That's sweet. I never thought what I did was impressive. If anything, I thought I was terrible at this, exiting visions with hardly any clues to hold on to. Our father always expected so much from me in the past, and I let him down every single time.

I drop my head to avoid Dylan's kind, soft eyes. I move my fingers from paper to paper, tracing pictures of dozens of missing girls. They're all young. It's the only detail that stands out. The oldest is twenty-two, the youngest the eight-year-old from the Amber Alert. I vaguely recall that one.

Our father always studies Amber Alerts. He reads the license plates on cars we pass on the road until an update is revealed. If a detail on a car has even a miniscule resemblance to the one described, he has me put my hands against the metal and wait for a revelation. I remember this case, because it was odd. The police had been following the lead that a family member abducted the girl because that was almost always the culprit in these cases. But another child had abducted her. Our father talked about it over dinner. My newest investigation consumed my thoughts at the time, and I didn't really listen.

"We can eliminate this one; It's been solved." I crumple the Amber Alert into a ball and drop it on the floor beside Dylan's backpack. "I don't recognize any of these other girls. They weren't the ones in my visions."

Dylan traces a finger along the jaw of the first missing poster: Ena Jones. "You see it too, right? They could be twins. Well, maybe not twins, but sisters. They could be sisters."

"I only saw one picture of Brit." I duck my head as a fly buzzes by with a high whine.

Dylan pulls a brown leather wallet from his back pocket. Tucked under his driver's license is a folded piece of paper. He carefully opens it up like a blooming flower and presses his fingers against the creases to flatten them.

It's Brit's missing poster.

It's not a photo taken close up on some random day, but her team photo. Her knees bend toward the camera. Her thighs lock in a squat. Her lips tilt up, exposing her teeth. I imagine the cameraman instructed her to say "Grr" instead of "Cheese." Braids climb her head into a twisty topknot. A yellow bruise stains the skin below her knee.

Last seen by her boyfriend heading home from a morning workout. She was wearing black sweatpants and a red hoodie.

"You were the last one to see her?" I ask.

Dylan tenses in the chair. "Yes. On the off season we go on runs together. There's this really nice trail. The view never gets old, you know? It was just another day, we did another run, and we were both planning to go home to shower and meet up for lunch, but then she never came. I didn't even know she was missing until the police showed up at my house."

"I thought you two weren't on the best terms by that time?"

Dylan nods and shifts in his seat. He twists the gold band around his finger repeatedly. "We met up for runs, but that was it. Not a lot of socializing during it, just movement, buddy system for safety outdoors, you know?"

I sit beside Dylan and swat away another fly that flashes past my ear. "It was the same every time? You always met up for lunch after?"

"We didn't meet up for lunch every time. We only planned that last time before she disappeared. I wanted to repair the relationship."

"Did you see anyone else on the trail? Or a car in the parking lot? Anything different or bizarre?"

"We both took a bus there and walked the rest of the way. The trail is easy, normally full of families with kids. But that day, it was just us."

Three flies dance above my head now. Their incessant buzzing makes it hard to focus on Dylan's words. I swat my hand aggressively above my head.

"Uh, you okay there?" Dylan asks. He leans back in his chair and studies the space above me. He holds Ena's picture in one hand and Brit's in the other. They couldn't be sisters. Maybe cousins. They have similar smiles and the same soft, almond-shaped eyes.

"I need to close the door. Too many bugs are getting in." More flies join the crowd now, weaving and bobbing around my head, always just out of sight, flashing past my peripherals. I jump up from my chair, sending it skidding backwards across the hardwood floor. I swat my hand back and forth in front of my face to protect my eyes as I turn for the open door.

"What bugs?"

"The stupid flies. It's like a horde."

The flies descend in front of my eyes like a black curtain. My foot catches in the arm strap of Dylan's backpack, and I crumple to the floor.

My knees dig into the sharp, itching points of yellow hay. Straw plasters my hand, glued there by sticky, brown grime.

The smell of waste and copper sits stale and heavy in the air. I choke on a dry heave and wipe the gunk onto my pants. They are denim jeans. A rip in the knee reveals dark skin, bruised and bloodied. *Who am I? Brit? One of the girls from the posters?*

Flies swarm, buzzing so loud it makes my brain feel like it's vibrating out of my skull.

Thick, wooden slatted walls create a square around me. The purple shade of a rising sun slithers through narrow slits between the boards. A metal gate with wide gaps in between the rows locks me in this small room.

I stand on trembling legs. The muscles ache, like after a rough workout. I wipe something crusty from my eyes.

A black cloud of flies dance among my legs, landing on my throbbing knee and a lump hiding in the shadows beside my bare feet.

A gasp escapes my lips, and I fall to the floor. I recognize this lump. Well, I don't, but the body I'm living through at the moment does.

My arms are leaden, heavy. The muscles groan as I reach for the thing beneath the flies. My fingernails are shredded and bloody at the tips. They ache with the rest of my weak body.

My hand rests on something soft. The movement doesn't threaten the flies; they continue to rove across the lump in a whining mass.

I pull a lighter from my pocket. It takes half a dozen clicks for the flame to ignite. Each scrape of my bruised fingertip against the metal starter sends a jolt of pain down my spine, forcing my jaw to clamp down.

I hold the light near the buzzing crowd.

Undulating flies part like curtains, revealing a tangle of wild blonde hair.

Red smudges leave my fingertips to stain the hair as I move it aside, revealing a face.

Bloodshot eyes stare wide at the ceiling. A fat, purple tongue escapes cracked lips. A deep, crusty gash runs across her forehead. Three sagging, torn puncture wounds pull on the skin of her eyebrow. *Not Brit. Another girl from the posters?*

I fold into myself. My forehead rests against the cold, lifeless hands of the body. Sobs shake my shoulders, pulling at tense, exhausted muscles.

Somehow, no tears come. I must be dehydrated. Or the shock is too much, and my body is doing everything in its power to stay alive.

I close the lid on the lighter and tuck it back into my pocket. I crawl towards the metal gate, dragging bits of hay with me. It itches where it pokes the wound on my exposed knee.

The gate swings open with a grinding moan.

I crawl from the stall into the open space of an empty barn.

A row of stalls mirror the ones behind me. Every gate is closed, and shadows hide the interiors. The buzz of flies only emanates from the one I left.

I use a wooden support beam to help myself stand.

I push off from the wall as I make my way across the barn.

In visions like this, I get caught up in the horrors of a dead person's last moments. It takes a lot of mental effort to focus on cataloguing everything I've seen. It's like lucid dreaming. I remind myself this is not me; I am not going through these horrible things. I need to take notes to handle the aftermath of what I see.

A board is loose below unmoving double doors. My fingertips sink perfectly into grooves etched there.

Short, high-pitched squeals ring out from wherever the door leads. I notice a smell here too. Unpleasant, and pungently earthy.

In between the wooden slats, I glimpse the fuzzy, pale pink bodies of pigs. Lots of pigs. Roaming free around the barn, napping lazily in the early sun, feasting on chunky slop with the occasional apple core and corn cob among the paste. They squeal again and charge out of eyesight.

A boot caked in mud steps into my view. The pigs surround my abductor, my best friend's killer, happily singing as he upends a bucket of moldy bread and brown banana peels into the trough. The pigs clamber over each other to reach new exotic delicacies.

Two boots turn into a pair of legs that squelch in the mud toward me.

I scurry away from the door, tripping and catching myself to run hunched over back to my stall.

Chains rattle before falling from door handles with a clink.

Footsteps crunch into the barn, snapping dried hay and sticks littering the floor.

I play dead, crumpling into a ball in the stall's corner. I clasp my hands together tightly against my stomach, urging them to stop shaking, begging them not to give me away.

He enters the stall and stops, standing over two still bodies.

I hold my breath. The lids of my eyes crinkle as I mash them closed.

Even though I cannot see him, I feel his eyes on me—studying my form—searching for a sign of movement, a sign of life. I will not give him one. I will not end up like my friend.

Hay shifts and slides around the stall as he shuffles forward, his boots never leaving the ground. Sharp, yellow points dig into my skin, infiltrate the knitted threads of my clothing.

He grunts as he lifts the body beside me. Her long, tangled hair brushes against my ankle as she rises. I twitch. It feels as lifeless as I would imagine. Wispy and thin like plastic doll hair.

His boots crunch away from me. I sneak an eye open as he exits the stall.

She is thrown over his shoulder like a sack of feed, or some other object without life. That's what she is now. An object. A body. No longer a person. Not my best friend. Not an adventurous, funny, beautiful girl. Just a thing. A dead thing to be thrown over a shoulder and disposed of.

I copy the man's earlier movements—shuffling my feet without lifting—to stand and exit the stall as well.

I only make it a few feet.

He's still in the barn.

He squats down, body limp across his shoulder, and searches among strewn hay for an object.

When I see a glint, a flash of silver, I bolt for the door.

I throw it open. Sturdy wood pounds against the outside of the barn.

The sun is a blinding beam in my eyes, disorientating me. I can hear the screaming of its heat—its brightness—as my eyes bounce around my surroundings like a stray ball.

Birds chirp in the trees around the barn. My heart beats up my throat into my ears. I stumble forward and my shin catches on something.

It's only when I look down that I notice I'm surrounded by fuzzy, pink creatures. They're the ones making so much sound, not the sun. They squeal and chitter, circling me.

The man lets out another grunt following the slam of a leaden body hitting wood floor.

I shove through the sea of pigs. They squeal louder as footsteps crunch from the barn into the pen with me.

I can't look back. If I look back, I die. I know this in the ancient, primitive way humans know things from their ancestors. Perhaps my great-great-great grandmother once found herself in a similar situation. Abducted and held in a barn with her dead best friend. Now, the memory is etched into my bones, into the twists of DNA helixes. If I look back, he wins.

I hop over a rickety wooden fence, the slats fuzzy from years of streaming rain and battering wind.

There is a decrepit house in the distance. The sun rises just over the shingled roof, creating a white halo. The house must be the man's. And the sun must be on his side, painting an angelic picture of something glaringly opposite.

I will not hide in that house, but I cannot hide in the trees surrounding us either. He will know the forest. He will have shortcuts and traps. A sudden, slender gap between dense foliage guarding the tree's trunks tells me not only the man, but other girls, have gone this way. I doubt they made it far.

I run past the trees and past the house. My lungs burn. The sun beats down, intending to boil my skin.

A dirt path, a real one, meant for a sturdy truck, cuts through the forest with a sharp turn. I can only hope this one leads to the highway where I can wave down a passing car.

She won't make it. My heart—Delilah's heart—falls. It's brutal, unbearable, to watch. To see how hard these girls fight, how scared they are, knowing they won't make it. I used to hope. I quickly learned not to.

I wouldn't be here, watching this escape attempt, if she made it out. She would be on the news. Her abductor would be in prison. She would write her story, tour talk shows, and warn other young girls about the dangers of strange men. She would attend a self defense class—maybe even teach one—if she made it to the highway. But she isn't. I've never heard of her before. The worst part is coming up, just around the sharp bend her body pulls her to.

I see the grey edges of a pebbled road as I round the turn.

Thick brambles cover this path. A car sits at the side of the road. Glossy black and white sheen brings a smile to my face. Someone out there noticed I was gone. They've come looking for me. They've found me.

I open my mouth, words dancing on the tip of my tongue.

Something crashes into the back of my head.

I fall forward.

My hands aren't fast enough to reach out and catch me in time.

My chin hits the dirt hard. I bite down on my tongue harder. Blood fills my mouth, drowning my words.

I spit onto the road. Frothy pink swirls around a hard white stone.

A hand grabs my hair and lifts me up. A grimace pulls my lips across my teeth. The jagged edge of my broken tooth cuts into the pink skin.

If I die, someone is going to know I'm here. I'll make sure of it.

"H–"

Cold metal drags across my windpipe, cutting my words short.

When I'm back to myself again, in my own body, I'm laying on my side. One arm cradles my head while my leg is bent forward, holding me in place.

When it became clear my visions were here to stay, our father took my brothers to a first aid training session at the nearest hospital. This isn't the first time I've returned from a vision in this position after a collapse.

The back of my head aches where I took a blow, and my chin itches. My arm is shaky and tired as I reach forward and feel a scab crusting over the skin there.

A hand moves to my arm to help me sit up. It's John. His cheeks are pink and his lips fall into a deep frown.

"Are you okay? Delilah, are you okay?"

I turn to find Conner holding Dylan back by the shoulders. My brother won't let him come near me. Dylan continues to push against

Conner, but they don't move. The force of two mountains pressing against one another. Conner must be in the higher weight group.

"Tell them I didn't do anything, Delilah," Dylan pleads. "They think I hurt you."

I hold my hand to my head, pressing into the space above my eye where my heartbeat pounds against my skull.

John throws open a cabinet to grab an empty glass and fills it with water.

I close my eyes and listen for the buzz of flies. There is none. There never was. Not here.

John sits on the floor cross-legged and hands me the glass of water. I down it in one swig.

I point to the table piled with loose and wrinkled papers. "Bring me those," I say to no one in particular.

Conner hesitates at first, but eventually steps away from Dylan and lets him gather the papers into a messy stack.

I sort through the pages. The words are fuzzy, but the pictures are clear. I drop the stack of papers to the side and hold one sheet in each hand. I hold up the picture of Ena Jones. "I think I experienced what happened to her."

The boys focus on the face on the missing poster. John's expression never changes, but both Dylan and Conner look defeated, the tense lines of their faces drooping, as the knowledge of what that means for her reaches their minds.

"And she was already dead," I say, holding up the other paper detailing the disappearance and last known whereabouts of Kathy Ray.

John, never fazed, asks all the questions while the others absorb the shock. "It feels inappropriate to drumroll this reveal. Who did it?"

"I don't know."

"Well, what did they look like?" John presses.

"Muddy boots. Denim pants. Um..." I hold my head in my hands while I think, bringing foggy memories to the surface. "A farmer, I think. Yeah. A farmer."

"So we're looking for someone wearing overalls and carrying a pitchfork? With a stalk of wheat hanging out of their mouth?"

"A pig farmer. There were pigs."

John makes a disgusted face, his lips peeling away from his teeth. "Do you remember any street names or special landmarks?"

"No need," Dylan chimes in. He bends down to pick up a paper discarded beside me on the floor. "There are only a few farms in the area, one in our town and two a few towns over. It would only take us an hour to hit all three. We could check them out and be back in time for lunch."

"That's not a good idea. We should tell the police, not go out there ourselves," John says without looking directly at Dylan. He takes my hands in his and helps me stand. I wobble, and Conner slips an arm around my shoulder.

"What could we tell the police without any evidence?" Conner asks.

"Anything it takes to get them there. We shouldn't be the ones investigating."

I break away from my brothers to hobble back to the table. My legs feel weak, bones stuffed with straw and hay like the barn floor. "We'll be more careful this time, John. It won't be like Ralph's."

"Careful isn't good enough."

"You afraid of pigs or something?" Dylan asks.

"Yes, I am, actually. As should everyone here be."

I slip into a chair and lay my head on the table, turned sideways to listen to my brother speak. My brain swims in a pool of dizziness.

"Do you know what pigs eat?" John asks. He holds up his hand as Dylan opens his mouth. "And don't guess something stupid like slop. I'm asking if you really know."

Dylan shrugs. Conner shakes his head.

"They eat anything. Do you know the definition of anything?"

"Any-thing, right? It's in the name. All-inclusive?" Dylan looks to Conner for help, but Conner watches me and supplies a reassuring smile that falls off his face a second later.

"Yes, and anything includes people."

I close my eyes and hold my stomach as acid sloshes at the thought. He was carrying the body from the barn. He could have been carrying the body anywhere, but why bury it where anyone could find it when his pigs could do the hard work and make all the evidence disappear.

"Oh no. Please, no." Conner's eyes grow wide, black pupils overtaking sky blue irises. "There was a menu at Ralph's, above the bar. They're famous locally for their bacon burgers, or so they advertise. I only remember because I was hungry, and it sounded good, and I wanted us to get some before we left, but then we couldn't. It said their bacon is locally bred and raised, and the pigs are pure-fed. I thought 'whatever that means,' but now I think I know what that means."

"According to this, we passed the barn on the drive to Ralph's," John says, reading a map he somehow acquired from Dylan.

"Should we bring anything with us? A first aid kit in case Brit is there?" Dylan's head swivels between all of us.

I close my eyes again and press the tips of my fingers to my temples. We can't send the police to the barn with no evidence. But if what John said is true—and it is, it always is—we might not want to step foot on the land lest the pigs be hungry for a fresh meal. And Brit won't be there. I could bet on it. She's been missing for a long time. If she was there, her body would have been fully digested and expelled weeks ago.

When I raise my head again, the headache slowly abating, all three boys are watching me. Dylan looks eager, hopeful. Conner stoic, supportive of whatever happens next. John doesn't have any emotion plastered to his face, but his eyes search mine, trying to open up a secret communication.

"What do you think, Lilah?" Conner asks. "What do you want to do?"

Conner's truck idles, pulled into a shallow ditch on the side of the road. The windows are rolled down, inviting a summer breeze to swoop through the seats and dance with our hair.

Ralph's Pit Stop is a mile down the road towards the South. We cannot see the decrepit corpse of a wooden farmhouse. Yet, the map says it's a quarter mile West into the forest. A dusty path carves its way through dense trees and thick underbrush, resembling the remnants of a long forgotten road.

A lone wooden post stands upright, splintered and sun damaged. The rusting head of a mailbox lies upside down beside the post. The plastic red flag is snapped off and missing, leaving behind a jagged stem.

A chill breeze infused with the scent of rain rustles the greenery around the path, bathed in shadow only a few steps in.

I've gained one clue from our arrival: none of the girls went to the farm willingly. The path is hard to find, for one, and ominous. Nobody would take this route on purpose.

Dark gray clouds, almost black, fill up the sky, shutting away the blue. I reach out and grab Dylan at the wrist. My fingers are cold against the warm veins that pump blood through his body.

"This seems like a good spot to mark on the map and turn into the proper authorities," John says.

Conner's hand hovers over keys rattling in the ignition, paralyzed before the final step of turning the truck off. "I think I might side with John on this one."

"Nobody has to come that doesn't want to." I pop open the door to slide off the backseat bench.

"Keep the getaway car running in case we encounter any killer pigs," Dylan says, lifting his eyebrows teasingly. He hops into place beside me.

"Those girls are already dead, Delilah," John says, sticking his head out the window. "There's nothing we can do."

I turn to face him. "In my vision, I—she was alive. One of them was alive. She may not be anymore," I shrug, "But if she is, or if there's another girl, I have to do something. I have to try."

John frowns. His mind is made up. It always is the second he makes a decision. He doesn't frown in contemplation, but in knowing we work the same way. My mind is made up too.

John holds his pointer finger up. "I'm not going because I agree with you or because I understand why you do what you do."

I smile at him, and Conner turns the keys to shut off the truck. Quiet sits in the air now that the rumble of the engine is gone. Not even the birds sing in the trees. Wind gently swishes branches on trees.

"I'm going because I don't trust this neanderthal."

Dylan throws his hands up. "Seriously? Still?"

"This could be an elaborate ruse to lure my gullible sister to your murder farm."

"That seems pretty elaborate," Conner says, joining the two of us standing at the side of the road.

John looks Dylan up and down, the pouting expression of disdain sitting on his face. "You can't trust anybody. Especially not a guy with a missing girlfriend that claims he has nothing to do with it."

Dylan lunges for the truck, moving in too close to John. John doesn't flinch.

"I'm here because I'm sick over my missing girlfriend," Dylan shouts.

John doesn't blink.

Conner moves beside Dylan to whisper in a low voice, "Step back and calm down."

"I'm here because I want to do everything in my power to find Brit, okay?" Dylan shrinks, retreating to my side. "I would never hurt her. I would never hurt anyone."

John slides out of his seat and closes the door behind him. "Whatever you say. If we have to split up, you're on your own."

Conner reaches down to pull the laces of his shoes tighter "Nobody's splitting up." He tugs the laces twice on each shoe before straightening—a nervous habit he picked up a few years ago.

Dylan snakes his fingers in between mine, holding my hand and taking the lead through the trees.

We emerge from the tree line to stand in a meadow of yellow, white, and purple flowers. They rise past my calves to tickle my knees.

The farmhouse isn't far from the path. It's as wide as our house, with a porch that follows the entire first floor in a square as well. The railing has fallen off along the front. Sanded wooden sticks tangle among tall grass.

The barn is further from the clearing, hidden behind the farmhouse, and set up against a line of tall, thick pine trees. Boards have soaked up the sun over several years, decades even. They change colors, a balayage gradient of brown to orange, orange to yellow, and yellow to white.

Tall grass invades the edges of both buildings. If I sat down among it, I would be lost, devoured by deep green stems.

I study the landscape as if I'm taking a picture with my eyes. This *could* be the place. But it was dark. The terrain was different, barren. There was no bright green life growing in my vision. It's been seasons, over a year. A lot could have changed in that time.

John takes a small notepad and pen from the front pocket of his white-and-gray, checkered button down. He tucks the cap on the back of the pen and writes. "Item One: No fence," he says, dragging out the 's' sound as he scribbles.

"I never said there would be a fence," I say. "I don't remember seeing one."

"Yes, but if I were a murderer, not that I ever would be, I would have a fence. In case my victims tried to escape. No fence."

"The barn was locked up with chains from the outside, right?" Dylan asks. "No need for a fence when your victims are that secure. There's no real chance of escape."

"A murderer wouldn't take a 'chance.' He'd have plenty of obstacles in the way were someone to escape."

"Alright, Johnny-boy the murder master. How about you explain to us how easily you stepped into the mind of a killer?"

John recaps the pen and tucks his notebook into his pocket. "Don't call me that."

Conner leans down to speak to me without the other two overhearing. "Why did we bring them again?"

"The more the merrier?"

John claps his hand on Conner's back. "Because three and a quarter heads are still better than one."

Dylan rolls his eyes. "How generous."

"You misunderstand," John says. "I'm one and a quarter."

"Alright, boys, before we get slaughtered by a man and his cannibal pigs, how about we quiet down and start looking around," I say. I step in front of the other three, volunteering to take the leader position from Conner for the first time in my life. This is my case, my crusade. It's only fair I'm the first to get eaten if it comes down to that.

"The pigs don't eat each other," John mutters under his breath. He retrieves his notepad again to scribble a question. "Cannibal pigs?"

"Delilah's right." Dylan stands beside me, looping his arm through mine and pulling me close. "Let's work together, use our inside voices, and look around."

Conner raises his hand. "Shouldn't we, I don't know, make sure we won't get shot for trespassing? Knock on the door? Make up a story for why we're here—lost dog or something? We don't want a *Texas Chainsaw Massacre* situation."

Dylan looks to me and I shrug. Conner is the movie buff, not me. John glares at Dylan, oblivious to anything our brother says.

Conner sighs. "A couple of friends needed gas for their car, walked all over this crazy family's property without asking, and got killed for it. Brutally, I should add."

"Sounds like they would have gotten killed no matter what if the family was crazy," Dylan says.

John slides the notepad and pen from his pocket again and writes. "*Texas Chainsaw Massacre* situation?"

I study the area. The farmhouse looms. Dried water droplets and dust from the wind stain the windows to create a thick brown film. "I don't think we should knock on the door and announce ourselves. We can keep to the edge of the property, with the trees, and sneak around back to the barn. That's really the only place I want to go."

John drops his hand, uncapped pen and notepad nestled in his palm. "What do we do if we get caught?"

Conner shrugs. "Run?"

"We won't get caught," I say, trampling the flowers at the edge of the meadow as I make my way forward.

Tall fir trees shade the barn with spindly branches. I can't tell if I'm relieved or apprehensive as my heart picks up speed at the sight of half a dozen pigs lazing under cool shadows. A fence wraps around their habitat, and a padlocked barn serves as a wall to lean against. This looks like the place I saw in my vision. But I—Ena was wounded. Traumatized. Terrified. My experience and observations were only as good as she could make in that moment.

"They're awfully quiet," Dylan says, watching two pigs dig their twitching noses into a trough of unidentifiable food.

"Pigs don't squeal just to squeal," John says. He stands far from the rotting wooden fence, chipped and riddled with holes. He brushes invisible dirt from the pressed legs of his black suit pants. "We aren't hurting them, or bringing food, so we may as well not exist."

Conner squats at the fence, searching through the board gaps at the trough. "Speaking of food, I don't see any limbs in here. Just vegetable scraps, and maybe some bread."

Dylan bends down beside Conner, both of them craning their necks to study every object in the trough.

John remains beside the trees, fiddling with his notebook and pen.

I throw one leg over the rickety fence, then the other, stepping inside the pigpen.

John jumps to the fence, his hands poised over the splintered wood. "Delilah, get out of there right now."

"Keep watch," I instruct. The pigs don't even bother to lift their heads as I pass. Does that mean something? Does it mean plenty of girls my age wander this way and the pigs are used to it? Does it mean I'm quiet and calm compared to the chaotic slaughter they see more often? Or does it mean nothing at all?

When I reach the barn doors, I trace the cool metal of thick chains looping, snakelike, around a lock with a hole for a key. I lean forward and press my forehead against the warm wood of the barn door. I blink an eye against the gap between boards until darkness takes shape.

A wide, empty space takes up the majority of the barn. Dirt covers the floor. If there is any blood staining the wooden boards underneath, I can't see from here.

I step away from the doors and walk to the right. I press my head against the barn again. Protruding wooden fuzz rubs against my jeans where my thigh presses into the fence. I wait for my vision to adjust to the darkness again.

From here, I'm looking into an empty stall.

It's not the stall Ena Jones woke up in, the features are backwards, but it is identical enough that I know this is the place. Kathy Ray died here. Ena Jones probably did too.

I spin around to find Dylan and Conner both beside me, looking through the slats as well.

John hasn't moved, and he hurriedly jots words and phrases in his notepad.

"We need to get out of here," I say. This is proof. Not any proof I can take to the police. At least, not yet. But I can use this information to protect other girls from ending up here while I find a real, tangible clue or piece of evidence to turn in.

"Not yet," Dylan counters. He breaks away from the barn while Conner holds his hand up to either side of his head to block the light and see better.

I walk up to John, pointing at his notepad and pen which he holds out to me. "This is what I saw. That's enough."

"What if there's someone in there?" Dylan asks, focus darting between me and the chained door. "What if Brit is in there?"

I find it unlikely anyone would be held there right now. There's no screaming for help for one thing, but there's also no blood. And the layer of dust and dirt on the floor of the barn is old. I don't believe anybody has walked across the floor in months.

"I don't think anyone is in there," I say. "I'm sorry."

Dylan grips the chains and pulls, the muscles of his upper arms hardening beneath his skin. "I'm not leaving until I know for sure."

"Delilah says we need to leave, so we're leaving," John says. He paces along the exterior of the fence, arms across his chest.

Dylan grits his teeth. He presses the sole of one boot against the barn door and pulls on the chain.

"Dylan, please. We need to go. We don't know if the killer is still around," I plead. I place my hand on Dylan's shoulder. The muscles ripple and grind underneath the thin cotton of his t-shirt.

Conner takes up a trailing link of chains in his hands. "He's right. We need to be sure no one is hurt. We can't walk away yet."

The wrestlers tug and huff against the chains. I hand John back his notebook and look around the pen. We need to break the metal. Pulling on it won't do a thing.

I turn at the sound of a crack.

The boys have pulled so hard, one of the door hinges has given up, allowing us entry.

I slip inside first. Conner and Dylan shuffle in close behind me. John remains outside, grievances on his lips.

My eyes adjust slowly, revealing the interior of the barn inch by inch. Dylan stands beside me, an arm protectively wrapped around my waist. Conner leans against the uninjured door, fighting to catch his breath among particles of grime and hay.

As I thought, dust covers the floor like a sheet. There aren't any footprints, any dragging indentations, any marks at all. The barn has been abandoned for some time. Long enough for evidence to lose its luster. Fingerprints will be worn to nothing—damaged by wind, rain, and age.

Conner straightens from the wall with an intake of air. "You were right, Lilah. Looks like nobody's been here for a while."

Dylan shakes his head. "It could be a trap to make us think nobody is here. We need to check every stall for Brit."

We're already here. We've already broken a door and breached the barrier. If nothing else, maybe we could find a clue. Something tangible to hand over.

We shuffle forward in a tight triangle, parting dust like mist. Dylan squeezes me into him. His arm is warm, comforting, solid. It bats away the chill and apprehension biting us from shaded corners.

We make our way from the main floor to the hallway leading to the stalls. Our shoes meet old straw, some plastered to the floor by grime. It doesn't look like blood, per se. The color is brown instead of red. The consistency sticky like wet tar.

There is no smell indicating anything happened here. Only dust and damp tickles our noses.

Each second we spend inside here instead of outside only makes me worry for John. He'd scream if someone showed up, but I don't like the idea of him alone among pigs that may have tasted human flesh before.

Conner pushes the nearest stall door open. The three of us jump back with a gasp and huddle together closer.

A heap of worn fabric—possibly a sheet—piles in the corner. From this angle, the mound looks to be the size of a body were it balled into itself in hiding. Or a corpse, chopped up and prepared for the pigs.

The lack of smell should be a relief, but it's not. Red splotches, lines, and loops stain the fabric. What was once white is now gray, bordering on brown. This sheet has been used countless times. But what did it cover?

Dylan finds a rusted pitchfork leaning against the wall behind us. He twists the wooden handle off and lets the metal prongs clatter to the floor.

He's braver than my brother and I. We cling to each other in a sideways hug.

Dylan lightly taps against the pile. The handle doesn't seem to meet resistance. Nothing stirs.

He inches the stick underneath a folded edge and gently lifts the fabric from the floor. Nobody hides underneath. Nor does a severed body part.

Conner releases pent up air from his lungs. "Oh, thank goodness." He laughs. "I thought for sure we were about to find a dead body."

"This is only the first stall," Dylan points out, literally pointing to the other stalls with the stick.

I startle when a shrill scream slices through the air.

Conner jumps back from me. "What? What's wrong?"

The scream rings out again followed by panicked words tearing a raw throat. "HELP ME! SOMEBODY HELP ME!"

I exit the barn in a flash, trailing dust behind me. I jump over the fence as Conner and Dylan exit as well, yelling something I can't hear. All I hear is the screaming.

My brothers are probably begging me to slow down, to not run into the woods blindly.

It's only as I push past the tree line, into the dense brush that reaches out with sharp fingers to try to catch my ankles and pull me down, I realize that voice may be screaming for help because she's being attacked. I don't have the strength or training to take down the burly men I've seen in my visions. I can only hope to spook them, or stall long enough for the boys to catch up to me, assuming they follow. They have to be. They wouldn't leave me alone out here.

The words haunting the air turn into unintelligible vowels—long A's that hold out like the breath of an opera singer.

I stop in a field shaded by tall trees and darkening clouds.

"HELP ME!"

"I'm here! I'm here!" I fold over, clutching my stomach. A cramp tangles itself in my ribs, forcing a wince for every intake of breath.

Conner reaches me first, placing a hand on my back. He's not out of breath. "What are you doing?"

"We need to find her. It's not too late. We can find her."

"Find who?" Dylan reaches us next. He places his hands on his hips and stretches back, face pointed up to the sky, sucking in gulps of air.

I strain my ears, listening as birds chirp in trees and insects buzz. "I don't hear her anymore, but it was around here. She's around here somewhere. Spread out."

Conner looks around. "Who?"

"I don't know, Conner, maybe the girl screaming bloody murder a minute ago," I snap. Useless. They're acting useless. Can't they see this is a crisis?

John reaches the meadow next. He's bunched up his sleeves to below his elbows and wipes sweat from his forehead with the back of his hand. "I hate to be the bearer of bad news, but we didn't hear any girl screaming."

I whirl around, facing each of the boys. "How could you n—" I close my mouth with a click of teeth.

An auditory vision. Rare. I've only ever had them twice before.

When I was young. Before our father came into the picture, and when our mother was still around. Whispers called to me from the basement of our house at the time, in a bigger city. In another instance, I heard crying from an empty bathroom stall in elementary school. Once my full-fledged visions kicked in, the ones where I'm powerless as I watch innocent people die, or bad people do the killing, I had assumed the auditory visions were gone for good. I was wrong.

I frown at Conner and whisper an apology.

He nods.

"What does that mean?" Dylan asks. "Was it a follow up of what you saw earlier?"

"It means, at some point in time, a girl was screaming somewhere out here," John clarifies.

"If I'm hearing it," I say, scanning the meadow, "then we should be looking for something."

Conner gets to work immediately, parting tall stalks of grass. "Any idea of what?"

I head toward the trees. So far, I haven't seen any girls lose their life in a clearing like this. They were always hidden among the trees. "Could be anything. A body. An item. A strand of hair."

Dylan joins Conner in checking among the grass. He even drops down to sink his fingers into dirt, brushing aside half buried rocks to search beneath them.

John returns his sleeves to their proper length and runs the palms of his hands down the now crinkled fabric. "Conner, watch for ticks. You're feeding your arms to them. And Dylan?"

Dylan raises his head.

"Carry on," John says before joining me at the edge of the meadow.

I smile and tap John's stomach with my elbow. "Play nice."

"He could be the one who murdered those girls."

"He really couldn't."

"He hired a lawyer. A good one. One who doesn't lose."

"He's protecting himself. And Dylan's dad hired the lawyer." I run my hands along tree trunks, feeling for some kind of mark or clue the girl may have left behind in case anyone came looking.

"Protecting himself from what? The truth?"

"We both know people in this town jump to conclusions. Just like you're doing right now."

"Found something!" Dylan calls out, holding up a green backpack crusted with mud.

I race to him as John mutters. "Of course *he* finds something."

Dylan doesn't need to open the bag. The zipper and its track have been ripped clean off, leaving behind a gaping smile with frayed thread for teeth. I stick my hand in and pull out a wallet. It's some kind of fake leather dyed purple. Inside are a few dollar bills, a stick of gum torn in half, and a driver's license with big bold letters spelling out **LEARNER'S PERMIT** along the bottom.

It's not Ena Jones, or Kathy Ray, or any other name I recognize. "Did we bring the missing flyers with us?"

Dylan positions the backpack over his shoulder. "They're back in the truck."

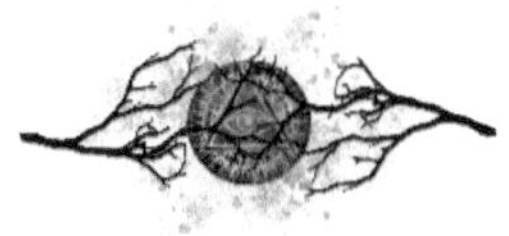

Conner drives us around town with no destination.

I didn't want to sift through the belongings of a missing girl at her possible place of murder where anyone could interrupt us, but I didn't want to go home either. Out here, I think better. And maybe—hopefully—I can trigger another vision of what happened to the girls at the pig farm.

Dylan and I sit at opposite ends of the backseat bench, our bodies pressed against the doors. We spread missing flyers out across the space between us. I didn't put my seatbelt on, there's no room, so Conner drives slowly and leaves large gaps in between the other vehicles while John huffs and sighs in the passenger seat at my disregard for safety. A guitar lightly strums on the radio and Conner bobs his head along with the beat.

I hold the ID up to compare to every missing flyer. No match. No resemblance anywhere, or similar names. This girl might as well be a ghost.

"What if she went missing recently? At the same time as Brit," Dylan says, taking the ID from me to do the same pass over.

I frown as he moves from picture to picture, not finding a match anywhere either. "It expired a year ago."

"Yeah, well, Jennifer Lowy, could have had it for a while and not been driving. Or she has a real license now and just didn't swap these out yet."

"Dylan, buddy," Conner says gently, watching through the rearview mirror, "I think you're trying too hard to find clues where there are none. We'll get stuck if we think like that."

I fish through the rest of the backpack. In my head, my brain repeats the same sentence: *she's already dead; you can't help,* while my heart fights to override the logic and begs me to believe we can still save Jennifer.

Dylan tucks the ID back into the wallet and drops them both in the backpack on top of crumpled gum wrappers and unopened packages of feminine products. The bag doesn't look like something to be taken on a hike or a camping trip. It's not sturdy, the fabric sheer, nearly see-through. This would be used for school, a stylistic choice over practical.

"Maybe she's not even missing," Dylan says.

John sighs louder and presses his forehead against the window.

"Think about it," Dylan continues, unbothered. "We're assuming the worst has happened to this girl. She could have lost her backpack. Or she could have left it behind to look like she's missing, but in reality she ran away."

"Projecting much?" John mutters.

"We should take it to the police. See if there's any connection to Brit."

"Veto," my brothers and I say at once. A smile actually cracks the statuesque stone of John's face.

"Veto? Like in politics? Really? Why?"

"It's messy to get the police involved when we don't have any crime to give them. Let's head home. I have somewhere else I want to check Jennifer's ID."

This investigation is proving to be difficult. Have I gone rusty from my time away? Or maybe I never truly had a knack for this sort of thing. Our father usually led the investigations he and I would embark on. He would bring special items, sealed in plastic evidence bags for me to bait a vision with. Or he would take me somewhere, midday when it was safe, to walk around. I thought I had been a co-investigator. A trusty partner. In reality, he might have let me believe that so I would keep helping him prove his clients' innocence.

Conner waits for another car to pass before pulling a quick U-turn that sends me hurtling across the flyers and into Dylan's side. "If you wanted to sit closer, you could have just said so," he says with a wink. A flutter ignites in my stomach, a warm, temporary distraction from my racing thoughts.

John turns around and slams his hand on the back of his seat. "Which is it? Do you miss your girlfriend or not? Because you're not acting like you do. You say you're sick over her disappearance while you move in on my sister. "

Dylan looks at John with eyes that smolder, as if he's channeling the sun. If John were an ant, he would burst into flames. "If I could trade places with Brit, wherever she is, I would."

John throws his hands into the air. I've never seen him gesture this wildly before. "Well, that settles it! You're a real knight in shining armor."

Dylan reaches forward to shove John's seat. It doesn't move. "What's your problem? You've had an issue with me from the start."

"No fighting in my car!" Conner grips the wheel tighter.

"We're on the same side here," I say, one hand pressed against Dylan's chest. I can feel his heartbeat through his shirt, a sturdy *thump thump* coming up to meet my palm. He eases back into his seat. "John, I've had several visions now. Dylan hasn't been in any of them. He has no motive for these murders."

"Thank you," Dylan shouts. He crosses his arms and gazes out the window.

John adjusts his glasses, pushing them up his nose. "You've never had a vision of Brit."

I move my hands to my lap. He's right. I can't deny that. I'm hoping my lack of Brit-influenced visions mean she's alive and well—living a happy life somewhere else.

Conner drives us home in an awkward silence accompanied by country music.

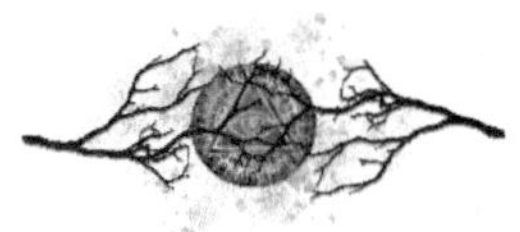

Back at the house, I lead the group again, doling out instructions. "Everyone look through school yearbooks in the towns near here. You can find them online. I'll take ours."

I find the last three years of high school yearbooks from Conner's room. They're the only reading material he has in there other than magazines with muddy trucks on the covers.

We sit around the table in the kitchen. The boys study their phone screens while I flip through pages. My fingertips move on their own to reach up and break open a scab crusting on my cheek. A bad habit of mine—picking at my skin until it bleeds. But my hands can't stay idle long. They're always buzzing with the same energy as my thoughts.

I don't find Jennifer Lowy in either yearbook. That doesn't prove nothing bad happened. It only proves she doesn't live here. She was a traveler. A vacationer. In the wrong place at the wrong time.

Dylan drops his phone in the center of the table screen up. "Found her!"

John widens his eyes at me, and I ignore him to study Dylan's findings.

Jennifer Lowy goes to a school two towns over. Her school is even smaller than ours—every grade and age meets in the same building. She should have been noticed. Her absence should have been reported. But she wasn't, and it isn't. John finds this after a quick search.

I don't know what else to do at this point. Ena Jones and Kathy Ray died despite others knowing something was wrong. Ena even thought she saw a police car right before she was tackled from behind. And people don't put up missing posters for girls that run away from home, do they? They put up posters when they know something is amiss. When behavior isn't expected, is out of character.

I'm in over my head. It took a trip to Ralph's and a visit to a murderous pig farm to realize it. I just got back from a mental health facility. Why did I think I could suddenly handle this kind of thing without a professional? Without a father who knows what steps to take and when it's time to involve the police?

The boys are looking at me, waiting for guidance.

John clears his throat. "What do we do now?"

I look at Jennifer's grainy yearbook photo. Braces stamp across the widest smile I've ever seen. Crinkles frame her eyes. I can't understand how anyone would want to hurt this girl. She looks harmless, kind, innocent. She should be alive. She should have another yearbook photo coming up—possibly one without braces and with a freshly straightened smile.

Maybe I'm getting ahead of myself. Maybe she is alive. She saw a mountain lion and dropped her bag and ran. Then the animal rooted through her backpack, stealing granola bars and destroying the zipper...

Now who's projecting.

I regard the boys. They haven't looked away from me. They don't want to make the call. I don't want to make the call. None of us should have to make this decision. This is summer break, and we're spending it catching two killers.

"I think it's time to take this to the police," I admit.

My brothers and I sit in a conference room, frigid with excessive air conditioning. Officers escorted Dylan to an interrogation room despite protests from me and Conner.

My older brother, tired of bouncing his leg up and down under the table, stands and paces the room. "Are we suspects? Why haven't they come in to ask us anything yet?"

"They're busy with the actual criminal right now," John says.

I lay my forehead down on the brown, shining, oval table. "He's probably terrified. We basically walked him into another accusation."

John pats my back. "If he wasn't guilty of something, he would have been released by now."

"Why are you so convinced he did something wrong?" Do they know something I don't? I would have thought being the seer of death and traumatic happenings, I'd have the answers, but maybe I'm too wrapped up in what I see in my symbolic third eye to decipher what my literal eyes see? Dylan has been beside me for most of my work on this case. I would have noticed if he did something suspect during that time. Right?

The double doors to the conference room open. A uniformed officer steps aside to reveal our father in a black suit and tie over a white button-down shirt. His normally tidy briefcase is clasped closed, but three sheets of loose paper escape the cracks, halfway out.

"Thank you, officer. We need privacy." He sets his briefcase on the floor under the table as his gray gaze settles on us.

John looks down to trace the smooth edge of the table. I stare back at our father, arms across my chest, goosebumps rising like a building wave across my skin.

Conner breaks the silence first. It's always Conner. "We can explain everything."

Our father slips the suit jacket off his shoulders. "No need. The officers informed me. Trespassing, breaking and entering. What were you thinking?"

He passes the jacket over the table, holding it in front of my eyes. I raise my eyebrows at him. It's a peace offering, and I don't want it. It's nothing, minimal compared to what he has to apologize for, to make up for. After our time together, I require a lifetime of peace offerings much grander than this.

Conner swivels his head between the two of us while John fiddles with a button on his shirt, slipping it in and out of its space, his eyes boring into the floor, his mind far away.

Conner takes the jacket from our father and slips it over his own shoulders. It's too small for his arms and leaves his upper body in an awkward, stiff posture. "Thanks, Dad. I was freezing."

"I'm disappointed in you, Conner. And you, John." Our father leans down, forcing John to make eye contact.

I grip the edges of my seat to keep myself from standing. "They did nothing wrong!"

Conner bows his head, his cheeks turning pink. "We're sorry. It won't happen again."

"No! You're not taking the blame. We didn't do anything wrong. We only did what *you* taught me to do," I stand now, pointing a finger at our father's expressionless face. "I'm investigating my visions, like always. Like *you've* had me do for years. 'For the betterment of our community,' remember?"

Our father's scrutiny darts to and from me quickly, disregarding my words. "You cannot enable your sister any longer."

I look to my brothers for comfort, but shame distorts their features, forces them to look anywhere but at me. "They were helping me because I asked them to. They tried to talk me out of it, and I wouldn't listen. If anything, they're the victims here."

Our father's voice mimics the gentle flow of undulating waves on a body of water. "Delilah, you are confused."

No. Absolutely not. He doesn't get to label me with that word. "I am not confused. I'm perfectly fine."

"You are sick. You aren't thinking clearly. You haven't been for a long time."

I scoff, and it sounds sharp, pricking and stabbing our father's eardrums. He blinks instead of wincing. "I'm thinking clearer than ever before," I say. It's a lie. He knows it as well as I do. I'm barely able to keep my head above water.

"Is that so?" Our father moves his briefcase from the floor to the table, unclasps the bronze lock, and pulls out the crinkled papers once sticking out from the interior. He drops the stack in front of me, and the pages fan out.

Each paper has my name, followed by Conner and John's, in bold and underlined type. Legal jargon makes up several sections labeled with various numbers and letters.

"Restraining orders," our father says, "from the man whose property you vandalized."

"Vandalized? That's a harsh word for walking around," I say. Okay, fine, I guess we pulled one of the barn doors off its hinges—a tiny, accidental modification to the building.

This is just another strike against the pig farmer I have yet to identify. I scan the document for his name. His signature loops along the bottom in textbook cursive font. *Benjamin Simms.* So this is the man I was meant to investigate. One of two behind missing girls and their undiscovered corpses.

"He could have taken you to court. He could have asked you serve a sentence in a youth facility. He could have done a lot worse. He would have had I not stepped in." Our father rips the papers from my hands to stuff back into his briefcase.

Conner and John continue to hang their heads, their eyes to the floor, accepting the reprimand.

"On top of that, you've dragged Dylan Walker into this mess, and he does face charges. You have made it very hard for his case against Brittany Hill." He says this last part to Conner and John, forcing them to take the shame and guilt that should be assigned to me.

"It's not their fault! I dragged them into it. All of them, including Dylan."

"I had thought your last investigation, and your time at Saint Anne's, deterred you from the complications of participating in the search for a missing girl. One that is clearly being handled by the authorities."

"Brit isn't the only one missing," Conner blurts out.

Our father sighs, emptying his lungs completely. "Delilah isn't the one who needs to figure that out. There is a team of people in this building who have studied this, who get paid to do this. Let them find the missing girls. Let them find Ms. Hill." He locks eyes with me. "Hear me when I say, there is no need for you to get involved. You cannot handle it. I'm asking you now to stop. I'm telling you all to stop."

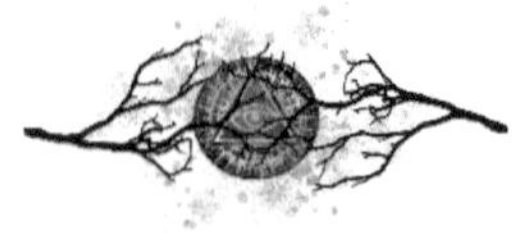

I find Dylan outside of the police station, sitting on a bench with his head in his hands. His frame trembles slightly. I sit beside him, awkwardly, unsure of what to do with my arms. Or myself in general.

Officers in beige uniforms pass by, pointing Dylan out to their partners and shaking their heads.

My hand hovers above his shoulders, but I think better of it and clasp my hands together in my lap. "I'm sorry," I whisper.

His shoulders cease shaking to tense. He looks up at me, the bottoms of his eyes glistening. "For what?"

"For putting you through another interrogation. How did it go?"

"Awful, but I don't blame you. I got involved for a reason, to find out the truth about what happened to Brit." He sits up and runs fingertips along the bottom of his eyes. "I don't regret it."

"Do they think Brit and the other girls are connected? Jennifer Lowy specifically?"

"No, no they don't." He shakes his head. "They think the incidents are unrelated and that I should stay out of this before it looks like I'm involved in more than one disappearance."

It's my turn to put my head in my hands, and rub the frustration from my face. I press my fingers into my cheekbones and drag downwards, leaving behind a dull ache deep inside my skin. "How could they possibly think that?"

Dylan shrugs. "Not a lot of suspects. Might as well pin this one on me too, right?"

"Not right. Not right at all."

I pause to watch a shadow move across the sidewalk as wispy, gray clouds steal away the sun. The sudden plunge into darkness sends a shiver up my spine, and goosebumps break across my arms. I suddenly wonder if I could trigger a vision here. I've done it before, when my abilities didn't feel so muted and hard to conjure—before a daily intake of medications numbed my senses mentally, physically, and now spiritually or whatever my bizarre abilities are credited to.

"Did they talk to you alone or did you have your lawyer?"

"You mean your father?" Dylan laughs as if I had forgotten their connection.

"Yeah, him."

"He was there for the tail end. Said they had no evidence and to release me."

I nod once.

"I got a restraining order from the farmer though. They made me sign it in the lobby, and he was yelling at your da—father."

"What did he look like?"

"Really young, which surprised me. He looked barely older than us, like a college kid. He was wearing a hoodie, ripped jeans, and nice sneakers. He didn't look like a pig farmer, let alone someone who feeds dead bodies to pigs."

"So then what makes you think he was the pig farmer?"

"Because he was yelling things like 'Tell your kids to stay off my property' and 'My family has already been through enough, we don't need this right now.'"

"What's his family been through?" I ask eagerly. This could be it, the clue we need to piece everything together.

"If I knew, I would have lead with that."

"His name is Benjamin Simms. Has anything happened in town with that name recently? He could be related to one of the missing girls."

Dylan shrugs and rifles through his backpack full of missing posters. "Simms...Simms. I don't remember seeing that name anywhere."

He hands me a stack of papers and I sort through them. No Simms anywhere, at least not in my pile.

Dylan shakes his head no as my family exits the police station. Somehow, John has gained a green sucker and our father holds John's notebook, flipping through the pages and skimming the notes scrawled within.

A man I recognize from my time solving past cases, but have never officially met, exits the station behind them. His uniform is the same style as the other officers, but his shirt is white rather than beige. He's easily the brawniest of the bunch. The moment he sees Dylan and I, he heads toward us.

Dylan notices and mutters under his breath, "here we go."

"Afternoon, Mr. Walker, Miss Dufort." The county sheriff takes off his brown-rimmed hat when he addresses me. He holds it in two hands in front of him. His thumbs run along the firm rim. "My deputies told me about what you and your brothers did. Trespassing on private property? Vandalism?"

Dylan sits up straighter, surprised and pleased a conversation isn't about him for once.

"I've already spoken to your brothers and your father about this," Sheriff Barrett continues, "And now I'm talking to you. What on God's green were you thinking?"

"Truthfully, sir, I don't know that we were thinking." I gaze up at the sheriff. "We were trying to help."

"I know that line of reasoning sounds noble, but it's not. It makes my team look like a bunch a jack-wagons that can't solve a simple missing persons case."

"I don't think this case is that simple."

Barrett drops a hand to his side. His hat nearly flutters to the ground with it. "And why not, Miss Dufort? You solve a lot of missing persons cases in your many years on the planet?"

I look down to avoid the burning irritation in his gaze. "No, but I couldn't help but notice the ID in the backpack we turned in doesn't belong to any missing person reported around here."

"Miss Due-fort," he sighs. "That just means the girl isn't missing."

I look up at the sheriff. "Respectfully, sir—"

He holds his free hand up. "You haven't been respectful this entire time, Miss Dufort. No need to start now."

I press my lips together. Is this what our father deals with anytime he brings forth evidence not originally on the radar? Hostility? Criticism for stirring up dust on a case already believed to be solved?

"What about the bullet I found?" I thought for sure bringing along my findings from octo-tree would be useful.

"Like my deputies already said when you turned it in, should take a few weeks to run ballistics. Considering you found it wedged in a tree and not a body, I don't think we'll find much."

I snap my fingers against my lap, and study the sheriff's shoes. Cowboy boots. Clean, polished, and shining despite the sun's departure.

"When we went to Ralph's—"

"So that was you?"

I resist the urge to look at Dylan for comfort. The last thing I want is to remind the sheriff he's here too, a part of this investigation. "I think they know something. The men at Ralph's."

Barrett shifts his shoes, toes pointed in different directions now instead of both facing me. "I'll look into it."

I raise my head as the sun returns, positioning itself behind Sheriff Barrett's body. I squint to see his face now, haloed by yellow.

"I'm keeping an eye on you, Miss Dufort," he says. "We need good girls around here, not bad ones." He walks back inside the station after a quick nod to Dylan.

Dylan opens his mouth, but he's interrupted before the words come out.

"Lilah, let's go!"

I sigh and reassure Dylan with a closed-mouthed smile. "I'll text you," I say.

We're not done here—with this investigation. The sheriff and his deputies clearly don't take this seriously. The only hope the girls have for justice, to be found, is from me. And I have a name now—Benjamin Simms. I don't think it's time to confront the pig farmer yet. I need more ammunition against him. I need more visions. I need to see everything that happened on that farm.

Dylan gives me a ride back to the farmhouse the next morning. After we all failed to convince the police something happened there, I knew this fell on my shoulders. If no one else was going to help these girls, I would. I was already their eyes and ears, what more was a voice?

As we near the unmarked path through thick brush, I pray Benjamin Simms can't hear the growling motor of the bike. I don't know what the punishment for violating a restraining order is, but I'm sure it's harsh. I can manage a little community service, or working off a fine, but Dylan can't handle another run-in with the police. I fear he's quickly climbing the list of suspects to hold the golden handcuffs at number one.

I hop off the warm, leather seat onto the road while Dylan shuts off the engine. He walks the bike in between thin, leafy bushes to hide it. I doubt the police force is unoccupied. Even Baneberry has the occasional case of petty theft, or speeding road-trippers passing through. There's not enough personnel to cycle this location into patrol on the off chance a couple teenagers come snooping around again. But, it's safer to be cautious—for Dylan's sake.

Dylan holds my hand and leads us through the dirt path to the farmhouse. My nerves wake up, tingling throughout my palm. My fingers quickly go numb, unsure of how else to react to this intimate gesture. My cheeks twinge, a smile growing rapidly.

Solving disappearances and murders together is anything but romantic. However, with Dylan, it feels special. Like we're devoted to each other, to this case together. Right now, it's the two of us against everything else. Our hearts beat to the same rhythm.

The farmhouse enters my view. I stop walking, tugging Dylan to my side. I could look at it every day, even in picture form, and the dread it brings would never lessen.

How many girls spent their last moments here?

How many saw that home, wished someone inside would come help, only to die? Screams and pleas unheard by anyone who didn't bask in them.

Now I regret camouflaging Dylan's bike. If something bad happens to us, if we don't make it out of here, we didn't leave behind a clue obvious enough to find.

Dylan slips off the path to huddle against a tree and yanks my arm with him. I gasp, nearly losing my footing.

"Sorry, didn't mean to be rough," he whispers against my ear, one hand still threaded in mine. He brings the other up to point past the farmhouse to the barn. "Looks like Ben is home today. Ridding himself of the evidence."

I follow his finger. Benjamin Simms leads pigs—one by one—into a white trailer hooked up to a truck. The pigs squeal and fight. They try to push past him into the open space around their small pen. He lets out a frustrated scream and kicks one of the pigs, sending it squealing into the trailer.

Dylan steps off the path. "Hey!"

Benjamin's head swings our way, and his body slowly follows. I try to press against the tree, but Dylan's grip is firm as he leads us toward a potential killer.

Any apprehension from before is gone. Dylan's wide, sturdy chest heaves. The veins up his arms bulge. "You can't kick animals, man. That's not okay."

Simms strides to us fast, a notch away from a sprint. "What are you doing here? I could have you arrested."

This situation is a fire pit with burning embers not fully extinguished. One wrong move, a gust of wind, a stick falling from a tree added to the pile, could set it ablaze again. I swing my body in front of Dylan.

"We don't want to cause any more trouble. We just want to talk." The words slip out, fast and oily. They steal all the saliva from my mouth. My tongue feels like sand, and my throat aches with dryness.

Simms takes a step back. No—he falls back as if I've slapped him. "Talk about what?" The tan from a life of outdoorsing has left his face, leaving it pale and slightly green.

I try to wet my tongue. It doesn't work. "We think something bad may have happened here."

Simms looks at me so long, I think he didn't hear me. Then he looks to Dylan. Then he laughs—a high-pitched mosquito sound. Almost like the squealing of pigs. The color returns to his face and then some, until it's bright red. "That's what you wanna talk about? Something bad happened here? Of course something bad happened here. My parents are dead. The house is trashed. I gotta sell these pigs, because I won't be spending my life taking care of them. Many bad things happened here."

This is it. Now or never. I say what needs to be said. "I'm talking about what happened in the barn."

Benjamin swallows, cutting his laugh short, as if I unplugged his voice box. "I don't know what you're talking about."

I study him. Fully, truly study him. Head to toe. He's tall. Not Dylan tall. Certainly not Conner tall. But tall enough to be the man in my visions. His width, however, does not look similar. He's lanky. A string bean like John. He can't even guide a pig into a trailer a few feet away. He couldn't haul dead weight around a barn over his shoulder. He couldn't heft a body over a fence and into a feeding trough. His eyes are blue, but dark—nighttime blue. When the sky is clear and the edge of a star's glow gives a glimpse of space beyond.

"How long ago did your parents die?"

Benjamin crosses his arms. They're riddled with scars. Small pink circles dot up to his elbows, incomplete games of connect-the-dots. "Why do you need to know that?"

Dylan notices the scars too. "Did they do that to you?"

Benjamin looks down and quickly drops his arms and presses them against his side. "Why are you here? If you're not here to apologize, then you need to leave."

"I apologize," I say. "We only trespassed because we think something happened in the barn. We think girls got hurt there."

Benjamin looks behind him at the barn. Only two pigs remain in the pen. They circle the area frantically. Benjamin has fixed the broken door. It's pushed back into place.

"We wanted to see for ourselves if there were girls in the barn before. If there were any left."

Benjamin sighs and shakes his head. "I haven't been here for a while. Not since my mom died about eight years ago. It was just my dad. Him and the pigs. He died a few months back."

I want to ask why he left, but I already know the answer to that question. It's painted across his forearms.

"I can tell you right now, when I showed up, there was nobody in the barn. And there hasn't been as long as I've been here. I don't know about before that, though. I would hope not, but—" he shrugs. "I wouldn't put it past him. To lock little girls up in a barn."

The three of us stand in silence. I've ruled out a suspect, but my biggest suspect now is a dead man. Could he have kidnapped Brit and killed her before he died? How do I get those answers now?

"Look," Benjamin sighs, "I'm leaving in a few days. You can come back and search around all you want after that. Just let me pack up some important things and go."

Dylan and I both nod.

We shuffle back out of the clearing as Benjamin returns to the pigs. I look back only once. He hangs his head. When he reaches the barn, he kicks the chained up door, falls to his knees, and holds his head in his hands.

Dylan pulls me against his side. The warmth of his body seeps through his t-shirt. It almost makes me feverish. "What now?"

Again with the 'what nows'. That phrase grates on my nerves. It's not Dylan's fault; he thinks I know what I'm doing—as do my brothers. Unfortunately, I'm clueless. My only lead is dead. It doesn't mean the pig farmer didn't kill those girls, but it does mean I'll never be able to find out his involvement. Not unless I find the second killer. Or Brit—alive— and able to give a witness statement.

I breathe in deeply through my nose. The citrus scent of wildflowers and the earthy tones of soil calm me. "I guess—now—we focus on Brit."

Dylan's arm tenses, pressing me deeper into his side. The faint echo of his thumping heart beats against my face. I can't imagine how difficult this next step will be for him. I'm nervous too, afraid we'll stumble into only bad news—a body or a vision of death.

"Can you take me there?"

We reach the bike, and Dylan throws a leg over the seat and slowly backs it from the bushes. "Where?"

"The last place you or anyone saw Brit. I think it's time for me to go, to see if a vision gives us anything to work with."

"This is it," Dylan says, gesturing with his arm at the parking lot and the dirt path ahead.

So far, nothing stands out to me as odd. This was the last place Dylan saw Brit. That doesn't necessarily mean she went missing from here, though. She could have gone home when it happened. Or been on her way to lunch plans.

"Is the parking lot usually this empty?" I ask, slowly turning in a circle to take in the area. Dylan's motorcycle is the only vehicle here. This place isn't hidden, or secret. It should be busier. Conner has walked this trail before. We've had school trips out here for picnics at the crest.

"Yep. Never seen a car here." Dylan waits by the trail marker—a thin plastic post once white is now slathered in crusted mud and hardened leaves.

"The trail isn't normally empty, just the parking lot?" Pieces of Brit's puzzle feel jagged, gnawed on by a young child or teething animal. None of them fit together.

"Yeah, I guess you could say that."

"I'm not saying that. It's what you told me a few days ago." I make my way over to a silver sign post. Pick-up times are posted in red across a fading white sign. I lean against the post, prepared to drop into a vision, as I run my fingertips along the numbers. Nothing happens. Disappointing, but the new norm for me.

Dylan laughs, impatiently tapping his foot against the packed dirt of the path. "You and John must both have those brains that can remember every little detail of every day that you've been alive."

"Eidetic memory? No, but I wish. It would make my volunteer-crime-solving job much easier." I walk the perimeter of the parking lot now, searching for any clue, any mark left behind. Even a thick, black tire mark in the road could tell me a lot, that someone rushed out of here in a hurry. A long shot after the time that's passed since Brit's disappearance, but a girl can still hope.

"You both took the bus here?" I ask.

"Yes."

"Why didn't you take your bike?" Dylan takes his bike everywhere. That could be a new behavior, however. Or the bike is new. Either way, I need every detail about that day. I need to know why he made each and every decision.

"Brit doesn't like the bike. She's afraid of falling off." Dylan tilts his head, looking me up and down. "I don't see what any of this has to do with her disappearance."

"Well, if you took the bus here together, didn't you take it back together?" I feel a rush of frustration building in my blood, heating it up and making the back of my head throb. Dylan's spoonfeeding me clues with an empty spoon. I'd rather he blurt out all he knows in one breath and then I can sift through the useless words to find the ones I need.

"She didn't want to wait for the bus, so she started walking. We finished our hike five minutes after the last pick-up. I waited forty minutes for the next one."

"And you didn't see her walking alongside the road when the bus drove back to town?"

Dylan tucks his hands into the front pockets of his jeans. "No, of course not. I would have said something to the police if I saw her."

"You didn't think it was weird—that you never saw her walking?"

"Not really," Dylan rocks back and forth on his heels. "I guess I figured she had made it home already."

"Why didn't you tell me any of this earlier?"

"It didn't seem relevant."

I stagger, halting where I stand, over a trio of empty glass beer bottles at the edge of the parking lot. Pink lipstick stains smudge two of the rims. "Everything about what happened that day is relevant, even if it doesn't seem like it. You need to tell me these things."

Dylan holds his hands up defensively at first, then moves them higher to block the sun as it breaks away from a prison of clouds. "I'm sorry. I'll tell you anything else I remember, I promise."

I shake my head. I try to not act like our father, full of irritation and impatience, but it's a skill I have to learn just like riding a bike, or practicing law. I tell myself it's not Dylan's fault. I didn't ask him the right questions from the start. I didn't push for answers.

I take a deep breath. How would our father get vital information—calmly, politely, professionally? I've endured enough interrogations, watched tapes, listened to recordings in the past. His trick was sympathy—or empathy? Is there a difference? He showed sympathy...I think. He used his voice, his face, to show compassion. People wanted to give every detail they could to a face like that—one that seemed to understand.

I address Dylan with a soft voice infused with concern. "This was the last place you or anyone saw Brit, but she could have gotten lost on her way home, or abducted."

"Or run away," Dylan adds.

"Or run away," I agree. "How many miles are between here and town?"

"Maybe five." Dylan sheds his backpack and sets it on the asphalt. "I brought a map with me."

He holds the map between us. It covers the tri-state area. Our town sits on the edge of the far west. I use my finger to trace circles around important points in the investigation: the pig farm, Ralph's, the meadow housing octo-tree. Last, I trace this parking lot, the hiking trail, and the stretch of forest with a two-lane road into town.

"It doesn't make any sense," I mutter, shaking my head.

"What doesn't?" Dylan watches my fingers dance between each point, searching for a connection I can't make.

"Look how close together these three are." I use my middle three fingers to cover each location.

"Now look at where we are now," I use the thumb of my other hand to cover the last point on the map. Technically, this trail isn't even a part of the tri-state—it's right on the line. The map doesn't care about what lies outside our bubble, so only half the name is visible.

"Okay..." Dylan drags out the 'ay' sound.

"Do you see the problem?"

"I mean, I guess this is a little farther than the others."

I remove my fingers, my hands falling limp to my sides. "Exactly. That's what doesn't make sense. If Brit went missing from this area, it's completely out of the way from where the other girls were taken or ended up. The ones that we know of, at least. There's no connection. Why is Brit's case different?"

"We're surrounded by trees. And she was—is—the same age as the other girls. Those are two glaringly obvious connections."

"Why would the pig farmer come all the way out here, to a normally busy hiking trail, just to abduct Brit? It's way too risky."

Dylan folds the map and tucks it into his backpack. "Maybe it wasn't planned. Maybe it was a crime of opportunity. He was driving, saw Brit walking alone on the side of the road, offered her a ride, and then..." he drops his head.

"I'm going to be honest, Dylan. With my, admittedly, limited expertise, I don't think Brit and these other girls have anything to do with each other. I think the only connection is that they went missing around the same time. Which isn't a connection, more like a coincidence."

Dylan nods, staring up at the sky, blinking building tears from his eyes.

"You know Brit more than me—you know what happened that day—so I'm going to proceed based on your answer."

Dylan closes his eyes, soaking up the sun on his face like a plant.

"Do you really, honestly, believe Brit would have run away?"

"No," he answers instantly, before the last word can finish falling from my lips.

"Not anymore," he adds. "I wanted to believe it, because I wanted to believe she was alive and well and nothing bad happened to her. But after reading those missing posters, visiting the pig farm, talking to the cops, I can't believe that anymore. I think someone hurt her. I want to find out who. I want them to be punished."

What I told Dylan is true: he knows Brit. He's the only one that knows what happened that day. Yet, the jagged puzzle pieces mock me as they refuse to fit into any comprehensible order—any big picture. My mind tells me Brit's disappearance is nothing more than a coincidence. But if she wouldn't have run away, who could have wanted to hurt her?

"We'll go forward with our investigation under the assumption Brit is a victim. Somebody took her."

Dylan digs his shoe tips in the dirt, creating a divot that unveils a few ants that scurry into the tree line.

"I'm sorry," I say. "That was probably difficult to admit."

"No, no. It's good that I finally came to terms with it. It's the only way to get her the justice she deserves."

I loop my arm around Dylan's back and squeeze him into my side. The gesture feels stiff coming from me. Conner is the one who's quick to gift out hugs when needed. John and I both feel physical contact is like a surgeon's blade cutting through our every nerve. "You can still have hope, you know? Brit could still be alive out there waiting for us to come find her."

Dylan curves an arm around me too. His fingers are cold and damp where they press into my side. "I hope so."

We waddle side-by-side back to the bike parked at the edge of the lot.

Originally, I wanted to hike the trail with Dylan. I even wore my nice running shoes with thick soles and pulled my hair up into two little buns at the top of my head. But the trail won't have any clues to help Brit if Dylan saw her leave it shortly before her disappearance. Plus, a hike that long is a waste of time when a girl's life might still be on the line. It's time to move to the next lead, the next location with an opportunity for a vision.

Maybe after we find Brit—dead or alive, hopefully alive; I pray she's alive—Dylan can take me on the hike. We can figure out a definition for our relationship. Discuss what we both want to be to each other.

I expel the thought from my mind with quick blinks. That's for Brit and Dylan to decide when the time is right. He's still hers. I'm only here to make sure they get that time, if I can.

"I still don't see why the pig farmer would have any reason to abduct Brit. Do you know of anyone that might have had it out for her? A previous bad breakup? A jealous friend? A rival athlete? Anyone?"

Dylan purses his lips as he thinks, removing his arm from around my side to hand me his spare helmet. "She didn't have any friends, and her only ex was from the fifth grade."

I run my thumb along the peeling heart sticker on the helmet. I wonder if Brit put it there. Or if Dylan did it for her, to make her more comfortable before she decided the bike was too frightening to ride. "Really? No friends at all?" I'm not sure why I'm surprised. I don't have any friends either. I guess I could count Dylan as a friend now. And my brothers are my best friends, but I can't really say that if someone asks 'who's your best friend' unless I'm prepared for judgemental facial expressions in response.

"Well, she had one friend, but they had a falling out months before Brit went missing."

"Over what?" I squash two buns flat against my head as I put on the helmet.

"I don't know. She never said." Dylan straddles the bike and dons his own protective wear. "You can ask her. See if she knows about anybody I don't. I doubt it, though. Maye Elliot. I think she lives in those colorful apartments right before the turnpike."

Brit and Maye Elliot had a falling out right before Brit's disappearance? How is she not suspect number one?

"Do you want to come with me?" I ask, looping my arms around Dylan's abdomen.

"I don't think that's a good idea. Everyone thinks I had something to do with it. I don't think she'll be much help if I'm there."

"I'll see if my brothers want to go. John can take notes." I smile at the thought. I wanted to give them a break after the trouble they got in with our father. I won't make them come with me, just extend the invitation in case they're ready to dive back into the case.

"Clear my name, alright, babe," Dylan says with a wink.

He kicks off against the dirt and sends us flying down the road.

My stomach flutters, sending jitters down my arms. I press against Dylan's back to steal the warmth from his t-shirt.

When we met at the ice cream parlor, he said his relationship with Brit was nearly dead by the time she went missing. Is it possible that once I clear his name, we can focus on our relationship? See if a title other than 'crime-solving partners' fits?

Delilah and Dylan. Silly, but cute. A sturdy name for a clever, new couple.

Maye Elliot lives on a third-floor unit at the far edge of the apartment building—in the green section.

She opens the door with apprehension—raised brows and pursed lips—when I knock. A towel wraps around her hair. Smudges of orange dye smear across her hairline. Her skin is dewy and clear, and she has the longest, darkest lashes I've ever seen lining down-turned eyes. She looks like a model. "Yeah?" she says, waiting for introductions.

"I'm Delilah and this is my brother Conner."

Conner politely lifts his hand in a salute type of wave.

"Alright," Maye says. She scratches underneath a splotch of dye on her forehead.

"I was wondering if I could ask you some questions about Brit? About her disappearance specifically?"

Maye pulls the door tight against her slender frame, blocking any visuals into the interior of the apartment. "Are you with the cops or something?"

"No. We're just people who want to help find out what happened to her." I shift my hands behind my back where I can rub my fingers together anxiously without looking like a conspiring movie villain.

Maye opens the door wider and steps aside. "Go to the last door on the left. I'll meet you there in a minute. I don't have much to tell you, though."

Conner follows as I locate Maye's bedroom. When we turn around, she slips into another room where I hear the echo of running water.

Her room has only a few pieces of key furniture, all piled high with cosmetic items. A heart-shaped wire box on her white dresser holds stacked and organized facial masks, hair masks, and boxes of perfectly aligned false nails and lashes. Fuzzy pillows and blankets in springtime pastels layer her bed. Each pillow is the shape of a different flower. I think I might be jealous of her room.

Conner steps off the soft, pink oval rug that is the centerpiece of the room. "Should we take off our shoes?"

"Don't bother. You won't be here long." Maye returns with the same towel, stained orange, draped around her shoulders. The soaked, dripping ends of her hair don't quite reach the fabric. She sits on the edge of her bed and gently glides a palm-sized brush through her hair. "What do you want to know?"

"Well, for starters, do you think Brit ran away?" I've never done this part before—the polite interrogation part. That was our father's speciality back when I helped him with his cases. I was simply there for the visions, to see if what the suspects said correlated with what I saw. I believe our father usually started with small talk and other pleasantries to establish trust. I skip that part, there's no time for it. Plus, I'm not sure what else to talk about other than questions about what I need to know.

Maye doesn't seem to mind my lack of true introductions and networking. She answers swiftly, still running a brush through her hair. "No. I know she didn't. She'd never run away."

"Respectfully," Conner says, "One of our sources said you two had some sort of falling out before Brit went missing. Is it possible you didn't know each other as well as you think you did?"

Maye rolls her eyes. "Let me guess: your source is Dylan?"

"He wants to find Brit. Find out what happened to her," I explain.

Maye puts the brush down, her wet hair straight, the ends brushed into points. "I can tell you what happened to her. Everyone in town can. He killed her."

"Again, with all due respect," Conner says, head ducking low, "we don't believe he did. We have reason to suspect an unidentified third party was involved."

Maye rolls her eyes again but doesn't argue.

"Was there anyone that had any reason to hurt Brit? A rival athlete or an ex?" I ask.

"Yeah," Maye's voice grows angry at our questioning. "Dylan!"

"Why would he want to hurt her?" I try my best not to sound skeptical when I ask, but it doesn't come out that way. My question feels sarcastic, like I wouldn't believe a word she says. It's hard to sound genuine when Dylan has helped with the investigation every step of the way. He was the one who brought Brit's case to me in the first place. Why would he kill his own girlfriend, then help investigate it? He wouldn't. No sane person who fears getting caught would do that.

"Dylan is controlling," Maye says. She walks over to her dresser topped with beauty products and opens up a cylinder of cream to smear across her already perfect face. "He has been since day one. They only started dating because he basically stalked her into submission."

Controlling isn't a word I would associate with Dylan. Perhaps he was like that at one point, but Brit's disappearance clearly changed him. He's been nothing but respectful and compassionate in our time together.

Conner's big brother instincts come out with Maye's description. "What did he do?"

"He would tell her what to eat and what not to eat under the guise that it was for weight requirements. He was always following her around school or when she went out with friends after. He'd randomly pop into our hang-outs just to check on her. It was weird." Maye takes a face roller to run along her forehead. Her perfect skin makes mine look even worse in comparison. Where Maye is dewy and clear, I'm splotchy with small red scars on my cheeks from endless skin picking.

I do my best to keep my tone neutral for this next question. Any inflection could be interpreted as blame. "Why did she stay with him?"

Maye sighs, setting down her roller. She turns to face me, but her gaze drops to the fluffy rug under my shoes. "I asked her that question so many times, but she never gave me an answer." Maye shakes her head, and when her gaze meets mine, there is a dam of tears building in her eyes. "I think she finally did it. I think she broke it off, and he retaliated. He killed her because I pushed her, and I wasn't there when she needed me."

I look away, blinking budding tears from my eyes too. This part is the worst: when I meet the loved ones left behind by the dead and sift through the aftermath of their emotions for the truth. Not that Maye is lying, but after we die, our friends and family look for all the signs they missed, signs that could have foretold the future. They find symbolism in even the smallest things, like the weather and what outfit the victim wore. They pick apart every interaction with every person the victim knew, pointing fingers at anybody that didn't say the right thing in those last moments.

I clear my throat. "Dylan told us the last time he saw Brit was after a hike. He took the bus with a plan to meet up with her later, but Brit didn't wait for the bus and walked back to town. Does this sound plausible?"

Maye shakes her head, and her shoulders tremble. "Not at all. Brit never ever would have put herself in a situation like that. And the trail they took was way too far, the city bus never even went that way. Her car was still parked in the driveway at home when she went missing. It's why she couldn't have run away. Dylan would have given her a ride. Which means he didn't give her a ride back."

I look at Conner then back at Maye with a shrug. "I visited the trail earlier today. There was a post to wait for the bus. They must have just added the route."

"You took the bus all the way over to Cliff's Edge Canyon?"

"Cliff's Edge?" Conner says, "That's, like, a forty-five minute drive."

Now it's my turn to shake my head. "No, that wasn't their normal hiking routine. Dylan took me to Kingsnake Trail." I trace my finger in the air, creating an invisible *S* similar to the shape of the path.

"Dylan lied," Maye says, pointer finger lifted. "That *was* their normal hiking routine when they first met. They'd been training for months for Cliff's Edge Canyon. Brit really wanted to do it—the trail— maybe as some kind of last hurrah before she finally dumped the guy."

I throw my hands behind my back to stop my fingers from picking at the little scabs already swarming my cheeks and forehead. I can't believe Dylan never told me any of this. Maybe it's not true and Maye is looking for a scapegoat—anyone to take the blame and give her closure? "Did you give this information to the police?"

Maye returns to her bed to perch on the edge, one leg tucked under her. "Of course. That garbage can of a sheriff said with no evidence, all he had was a," she brings up her fingers to bend into air quotes, "he said-she said situation."

My stomach feels queasy, a horrible notification I'm about to figure out the truth while being assaulted by visions. When I turn my head to look at Conner, he's already watching me, waiting for my next instruction.

If Maye is telling the truth, and Brit and Dylan really did go to another trail, I would be able to pick up clues the police never could. It would explain why I didn't see anything where Dylan took me earlier today, why interacting with the bus post didn't trigger anything. Not that triggering a vision really works for me anymore.

I clutch my stomach as I ask Conner, "Do you think we could make it there and back before dark?"

Conner makes us stop at home to change into boots capable of the first half mile of Cliff's Edge Canyon's strenuous hike. The total loop around the canyon is approximately twelve miles of rocky dips and curves. I hope if anything happened—not that I hope something did—it was at the start of the trail and not at the scenic point around mile seven. My hardly worn hiking boots can only do so much when I'm miserably out of shape.

I spend the drive picking at some kind of bump on my clavicle, tearing my skin and leaving behind a scab three times larger than the bump ever was.

I only stop when Conner's truck engine shuts off, and I realize we've reached our destination. Two other cars sit in the gravel circle before a trail marker and large billboard full of animal and plant pamphlets and emergency numbers. Everything is wet, incapable of air drying in the breezy mountains.

"It rained recently," Conner says, pointing to the wet surroundings I had been admiring. "I hope the trail isn't muddy, or else I'll have to do that fireman carry thing, and I don't think that's useful for your visions."

His attempt at a joke helps my petrified face to crack along the bottom, revealing a small smile. "I feel like I'm going to vomit," I say aloud. I'm not sure who I'm confiding in, but the feeling is so strong I need to vocalize it.

"Do you want to come back another day?"

"No, I need to do this. I need to know what happened. After talking to Maye, I've had this horrible gut feeling Dylan isn't who he says he is. He isn't telling me everything about that day."

"Why would he want us to investigate then?"

"I don't know."

We exit the truck, and Conner picks up each of the two pamphlets on the bulletin board and flips through them. A triangle roof over the information kept them safe from disintegrating due to downpour, but water droplets still cling to paper covers, smearing colorful ink and staining Conner's hands. "Lots of snakes here, but as long as we stay on the trail we should be fine. Lots of edible flowers too in case you're stuck out here for a night. Not that starving to death is ever the first worry if that happens."

He waits for me to respond. I don't. I hold two hands against my stomach, urging the sick feeling to go away.

"Because of the elements," Conner continues. "The elements will kill you first. Freezing to death is the deadliest one."

"Can we start, please? I want to get this over with." I can talk all I want, but I can't take the first steps onto that trail. Onto the place Brit might have died. I need somebody else to pass through the barrier, and I can follow.

Conner hands me the pamphlets and I stuff them into my back pockets without even looking at them. He holds his hand out for me to take, and I raise an eyebrow.

"We can do this together, Lilah. You're not alone."

Our steps squelch along the path. I grab onto the back of Conner's shirt to keep from falling during dips in the trail.

Laughter up ahead alerts me. Other hikers must be making their way back now that the rain has stopped.

When we turn to a ridge with a beautiful view of the dense forest below, there are no other hikers. I can still hear the laughter on the wind. It twirls around me, making me dizzy, before falling from the peak.

"Oh no," I whisper.

Conner rushes to my side. "What's wrong? Did you see something? Are you seeing something right now?"

A wail shoots up from the steep drop to my right. Mother nature herself screams at me. Warning me? Or recounting what she saw?

My legs give out and I slump against Conner.

Tears fill my eyes quicker than I can blink them back. "I can feel it— a vision is coming. I'm not ready. I don't want it. I want to leave. I want to go home."

Conner sits, bringing my limp body with him until we're safely sucked into mud. "I'm right here, Lilah. It's okay. I'm not going anywhere. I'll be here when you get back."

The memory clouds over my pupils like a shadow.

The forest looks the same. Tragedy never disrupts the trees. After countless disasters they're powerless to stop, they're no longer fazed. They sway in the breeze, allow whispers to carry through their leaves, but that is all they do—witness.

I stand near a cliffside. The wind up this high is almost unbearable. A shiver coaxes bumps up my arms and down my legs, hidden in thick black leggings. I untie a red hoodie from around my hips to tug over my head.

I reach down to pluck a fallen acorn from the ground. It's hard and cold in my hand, and somehow, I know my heart is the same—unfeeling— hiding deep beneath my ribcage.

I thought the serene atmosphere would make this conversation easier. A place of beautiful closure for both of us. It doesn't. Now we're isolated. The cold makes us retreat inward, seeking warmth from ourselves instead of each other.

"What did you say?"

I turn to find Dylan staring at me. His hair is long, shaggy, unwashed and unstyled from cold wind and the humid parts of the early trail. One leg is higher than the other, resting atop a flat stone. He holds a water bottle halfway to his parted lips. His eyebrows are raised. If he doesn't drop them, he'll burn white marks into the wrinkles of his forehead. He can still get a sunburn in the cold.

"Because," Dylan continues, "I think you just said you wanna break up. But that can't be what you said. It can't."

I make my way to Dylan and hold my hands out to grasp his, but he wraps them both around his stainless-steel bottle. "That is what I said."

"Why?"

The creases across Dylan's forehead worry me, and I want to reach up and smooth them out with my fingertips. I still love him, even if it isn't the type of love I should have as his girlfriend. Or maybe it isn't love anymore, but obligation. I still need to care for him while we're together. Until our hike is over and we go our separate ways, leading separate lives until we can only barely remember each other's names and that we once felt *something* close to love.

"We've been putting this conversation off for a while now, but we both knew it was coming." The words don't hurt me. They shouldn't hurt him. I've finished my high school journey. He's not far behind. I'll be going to a school hundreds of miles away. He will do whatever he decides to do once the time comes. This end is inevitable.

"I never knew this was coming. I never thought we'd have this conversation." Dylan shakes his head. I think he's forgotten he's holding the bottle, because he doesn't drop it, or help it continue its journey to his lips.

"Dyl, c'mon," I say. We've grown apart the last few months, this whole school year. It wasn't just on my end, but on his as well. This breakup was slow—it's been happening for nearly six months.

"You, c'mon," Dylan snaps, dropping his hand and bottle hostage to his side. "Where is this coming from? Did—" Dylan shakes his head as he thinks "—Did Maye tell you to break up with me?"

I laugh and fold my arms across my chest. "Of course not. This is between you and me."

"She's a terrible influence, you know." Dylan sets his bottle on the rock and steps down from it.

My brows furrow, creating burnable creases across my forehead too. "I can make my own decisions, and I have. We have very, very different futures ahead of us. The relationship isn't going to work."

"Not if you just give up on it like that. We have to work together, Brit. We have to try. Long distance won't be too bad if it's only for a few years. We can take turns visiting each other over the holidays, and—"

"It's not worth it," I sigh.

Dylan's mouth hangs open. "Why not?"

My flustered tongue dries in my mouth. Why is he making this so difficult? I thought this conversation was obvious. We were supposed to have an amiable talk, come to a quick and easy—mutual—understanding, finish our hike, and happily depart.

"Because this isn't...real." The word feels wrong, too aloof, but it's the only one I can summon at the moment.

"Real? Our relationship isn't real?" Dylan's heartbreak blows away with a strong gust that makes my legs wobble.

"You know what I mean. It was never going to last."

"Brit, what the hell? How long have you felt this way?"

I throw up my hands. "Since the start! I thought you felt the same."

"I did not feel the same. I love you. I always have."

I groan and drop my head in my hands. "There's no point in fighting over this. It's done. It's over. After this, we won't be together anymore."

Dylan walks toward me. "You can't give up on us just like that. No warning? No debate? That's not fair."

I never noticed before how tall Dylan really is. I noticed it when I first met him. His height, his strong, muscular build. The way he rises over me and I feel like a fairy beside him, small and cared for, despite my own muscular frame. The cold and the shadows that dance across his face from the swaying leaves above us turn those traits sour. He's tall.

Too tall. He towers over me, and I can barely read his darkened face. His arms are as thick as the skull encapsulating my brain. Those hands I loved to hold—loved to watch swallow mine as we walked down the hallways at school—are too big now. They're clenched in tight balls. The chest I loved to lay my head on and dream heaves with shallow breaths.

I take a step back as the first droplets of tears sting the corners of my eyes. "Dylan, I'm sorry. I'm so sorry. I thought this was going to be mutual. I didn't realize you didn't feel the same way."

Clouds pass over the sun, blocking the little rays of warmth and light we had. The forest stills. All the animals and singing bugs hold their breath as they watch Dylan. He stomps up and grabs my wrist. My knees buckle.

"Stop it. You're hurting me!" I cry.

"You can't just walk away from me, Brit. That's not how this works!" He screams the words into my ear. I nod as tears collect on my chin.

"Now, you're going to sit down and talk to me. We're going to work this out."

Dylan swings my body with a powerful swish of his arm. He aims for the rock where his water bottle keeps the seat warm. But he's too strong, too powerful.

As his grip leaves my wrist, I stumble.

I fall backward, watching through the trees as clouds finish their journey across the sun. I turn my head and close my eyes, protecting them from the bright, burning rays. My head hits something hard and I feel the crack as I hear it—a whip through the still silence.

Dylan screams my name.

My eyes remain closed.

When I open them again, I'm looking up at a cloudless sky. The tree branches are gone. Or they've parted for me. Everything is gray. Pure gray.

Something small brushes against my nose. I can't raise my arm to move it away. My limbs are weak, heavy.

I scrunch up my nose, and the small thing falls down the side of my face to join a pile building alongside my head and trickling into my ear. Whatever it is, it cradles my neck. It's warm and soft, insulating me from the chill of the mountain breeze.

Dylan's voice carries to me in a whisper. My eyes jut side to side, but I cannot see him.

"I'm sorry. I'm sorry. I'm sorry." I've never heard him cry before but that has to be the sound he makes. A whimper in between each word.

I open my mouth to say *I'm okay, it's okay, we can fix this,* but I can't. The words are stuck in my throat like phlegm.

I try to raise my hand to wave to him, but the very tips of my fingers only twitch.

More insulation piles down on me, covering my hands in something soft yet scratchy. It falls between my fingertips. I caress it. Is this dirt? Why is dirt falling on me?

Another pile pelts my stomach.

Then another hits me in the face.

It floods my nose and settles in the back of my throat. It burns.

My mouth makes fishy movements, but there is no power to eradicate the infiltration.

My throat swirls the dirt like a coffee grinder as I choke on his name. "Dyl. Dyl." It's not even a whisper, only the mouth movements.

Another pile fills my eyes. My tears make it worse, turning the soil into mud that films over.

I wave my fingers to signal help, but they're buried under piles of heavy dirt.

I open my mouth again, drinking in fresh air—enough to produce a scream—when another pile forces its way between my lips. Too much to close my mouth. My teeth bite down on an endless stream of earth.

When I breathe in, dirt follows. No air. There is no air. *Dyl. Dyl. I need air.*

I frantically gasp and find myself sitting against a tree trunk. Conner kneels beside me with panicked eyes. "You're okay. It's okay. Breathe, Lilah. You need to breathe."

My lungs fill and empty so quickly, a painful knot forms at my side. I wince and press a hand against it.

"You—you were in a trance," Conner stutters, his hands raising and lowering to mimic deep breaths for me to follow. "Then you held your breath. You just—just stopped breathing. Your face turned blue."

Tears spill down my cheeks. These visions are the worst—the ones I'm so deeply affected by. I can't investigate alone no matter how much I wish I didn't need to drag everyone around me into these tragedies. It's too dangerous for me, especially now that I have less control over them than before.

Conner follows his own examples until we're breathing in sync like yoga instructors. In. Out. In. Out.

My lungs finally catch up. The burn lessens. The vision, what I experienced, becomes clear. Dylan lied.

"What did you see? Did you see Brit?"

When Conner and I return home, I immediately retire to my room without a word to him of what I saw. I don't know if I can even stomach the words, if they can leave my mouth without bringing vomit with them. I can't sit on this information, though. I won't. Dylan will be held accountable. But who do I tell, and how?

Our father handled this part before—using the information we gathered to find the proper criminal. And does he know? Did Dylan tell our father the truth when he took on his charges? Or is he sitting in the dark, innocent and blind like I was only a day ago?

I pace my room and pick at the scab on my chin. I can't help it. My hands cannot be idle. My window has a clear view of the driveway, where I watch and wait for our father to return home. I can bring him this information. He can organize the next steps. Either drop Dylan as a client or turn him in. There has to be something he can do.

After an hour, when the skin on my chin is red and bloody, somebody else drives up. I hear the roar of the motorbike engine before I see Dylan reach the house with a trail of dust behind him.

My heart picks up speed. Why is he here? How does he even know I'm back? Has he come to explain? To kill me too?

I watch from my bedroom window as Dylan climbs the porch and knocks on the door. Surely, my brothers won't let him in. John never answers the door. And Conner can tell I'm distressed—a confused wreck of myself.

One of the boys lets Dylan inside. I hear his boots pound against the stairs in a hurry. I want to scream at him to stay back, to leave, but that is a guarantee to get myself hurt. Brit noticed it right before she died. He's strong. I'm weak. He could kill me with the same endurance requirement as a sit up.

I stand far from the door, my back pressed against my dresser, when Dylan gently raps against the wood three times. What do I do? I can't let him in, but he knows I'm here. *What do I do?*

"Delilah, can I come in?" His voice is soft, with a lilt, a singsong. He knows I know. He has to know I know.

He enters the room, opening the door just enough to slip his body through. He stares at me with furrowed brows. "Are you avoiding me?"

"No, why would you think that?" *Scatterbrain.* I hid in my room silently, hoping he'd either give up and leave, or someone else would tell him to. Of course I'm avoiding him.

"Why are you looking at me like that?"

I scramble my features, pulling each piece of me back into place, happy—no, not happy—what did I feel before I found out what Dylan did? I settle on what I hope is a normal look, resting Delilah face.

"Why are you looking at me like you're suddenly terrified of me?"

I shake my head, scrambling my features again, and plant a false smile on my face. It must not be convincing, as Dylan's frown deepens. "I just don't want another fight with our father, that's all. You should go before he gets home and sees your bike."

I try to sit on the edge of my bed, feigning a casual stance, but my hands tremble and my chin quivers as Brit's last moment's flash across my vision, layering my room with trees, dirt, and Dylan's terrifying face before he hurt her.

Dylan pushes my bedroom door closed behind him and advances deeper into the room. "Your father, huh? Well, I came by earlier, but John said you and Conner were out. He wouldn't tell me where. Did you talk to Maye?"

"Yep." I smile again and mentally chastise myself for my horrible, grieving appearance. Dylan and I have spent enough time together for him to know when I'm recovering from a vision. My eyes are probably sunken in, surrounded by black circles. Though that is starting to become my normal look, so maybe it isn't too off-putting.

"Okay, and?" Dylan sits beside me and it takes every ounce of control not to flinch.

"Was a waste of time just like you thought." I act nonchalant as I lean away from Dylan to press my back against the wall, as if I need the support.

"Did she say I did anything?"

"Well, yeah," I laugh, fake and whiny. "But she has nothing on you so..."

"So you left and went where?"

"You know, just hung out," I shrug.

"You just hung out? You and Conner...without John? And while you're investigating murders and disappearances?"

I slide off the bed and walk to where I left my cellphone on the desk. I swipe past dozens of missed texts over the last few hours from Dylan to unveil several message bubbles from Conner.

Dylan's here to talk to you. I sent him upstairs. Didn't tell him anything. Figured you would.

I hope that was okay, sending Dylan to you. Tell me if you need anything.

I casually tap out a message to Conner as I talk. "Even amateur detectives need a day off." The laugh I force out afterwards sounds so falsified, Dylan slides off the bed to join me. I press the sleep button on my phone and place it back on the dresser, screen down.

"You're acting weird, and you were clearly avoiding me. You can tell me what happened, you know," Dylan says. He wraps his arms around my waist and hugs me from behind. My entire body stiffens. He knows. He's joining me in this awkward game of 'act natural,' and we're both terrible at it.

He continues, "You can tell me what Maye said. I'm sure it was all lies, and I can ease your fears."

He's gentle, but strong, as he turns me around to face him by my hips. He stares into my eyes, seeing past the viscous nucleons to study my soul. "What happened, Delilah? Please tell me." He tucks a strand of hair behind my ears. His fingertips drag from my ear down my throat. It's meant to be romantic, an affectionate, heartfelt gesture, but it turns my stomach and makes me want to scream.

I plant both palms against his chest and shove him back. It's like trying to shove a block of concrete. He steps back once, in surprise, not because I actually hurt him.

"You killed her...you killed..." I hate that weakness infuses my voice as I face this monster. I wish I was strong like Conner, able to stand up and speak confidently. I wish I was detached like John, never losing control of my tone because of how I feel inside. But I'm not my brothers. I'm not strong like them. I'm weak Delilah, who cries as she confronts a murderer.

Dylan's eyes widen, and he brings his palms together in a pleading gesture. "It was an accident. I swear on my life it was an accident."

"I saw the whole thing! You could have let her walk away. You could have walked away yourself. But you killed her!"

"I know. I know. But I didn't mean to, I swear. She was gonna dump me—did you see that? She wanted to give up on us. She said our relationship was fake. She didn't even care about me!"

My chin trembles, making my torn open scab itch and ache. "How could you...you pretended like you didn't know this whole time. You made me believe in you. You made me like you!"

Dylan steps closer, tears mirroring mine. "I like you too, Delilah. Things would never happen like that with us. We're different. You're better than her."

"You're a monster."

Dylan looks between the window behind me and the door behind him. "Can you keep this a secret? Just between us. Nobody else can know."

I shake my head. "I'm not letting you get away with this. You're going to answer for everything you did to her."

"I have a scholarship, Delilah," he says with words so soft it's as if he's asking me to keep a secret that he sneaks out sometimes—not that he's a murderer. That he buried a body, covered his tracks, and lied to everyone he knew.

"And my dad—he's strict. He's so strict. If you met him you'd understand. Here—come with me. I'll show you. You just have to meet him." Dylan wraps his fingers around my wrist. Just like he did with Brit.

I yank my arm from his grasp and stumble back. It's almost like what happened to Brit, but this time, I have a flat wall to protect me from any sharp protrusions.

I hold my arm against my chest protectively. Red lines materialize on the surface of my wrist.

If this conversation occurred anywhere else, I would be dead too. The only thing protecting me is that Conner and John are in the same house, just a few rooms away.

"You buried her alive," I say. "Did you know that? You tortured her!"

Dylan presses the palms of his hands against his ears. "No, I didn't. She hit her head. I had to hide her body, but she was already dead. She wasn't breathing. I couldn't find a heartbeat."

Dylan blurs into a smudge of colors as tears clog my eyes. "Dirt filled her mouth. She couldn't talk. Couldn't scream. She cried and choked on your name while you threw more dirt on top of her."

Dylan closes in on me, his chest against mine, forcing my back against the wall. "She was already dead."

My bedroom door bursts open, the handle crunching through plaster to leave a spherical hole in the wall. Conner stands in the doorway. John hides behind him, a stethoscope set around his neck.

Tears prick the corners of my eyes. They've been here, listening, watching out for me.

"Time to go, Dylan," Conner says. His arms are across his chest in a way that makes the upper muscles bulge.

"We're not done talking," Dylan snaps without turning around.

John steps out from behind Conner. "You are now."

Dylan must realize he's outnumbered. He backs away from me and looks at the three of us—sees us for the first time.

"It was one mistake," he whispers so only I can hear him. His eyes are wide and pleading, a veil of tears building across them. "Please don't ruin my life over one mistake."

"At least you still have your life."

Dylan nods once and wipes his eyes.

Conner and John escort him to the front door. I don't move, not even a muscle twitch, until I hear the growl of an engine and the whine of retreat.

I turn and watch through my bedroom window as a pristine black vehicle rumbles up the driveway moments after Dylan's bike vanishes. I take a few minutes to wipe tears from my face with my hands.

My brothers watch at the bottom of the stairs as I make my way to our father's office, entering as he settles down for an evening of paperwork.

Our father sets his pen down on the desk when I hover in the doorway. It's a straight line, a ruler underlining the sentence he was in the middle of reading. He expects this conversation to be short, and he'll return to the line he left off on in just a few seconds.

I wish he didn't set his pen down that way. I wish he dropped it on the desk or threw it aside. I wish he didn't need to take the time to think about and measure his movements before he regarded me. I wish he was the way fathers are supposed to be—dropping anything and everything when they see their children in distress.

Fresh tears carve cold, shining crevasses down my cheeks.

He doesn't even ask what's wrong? What happened? Who hurt you? What can I do? He waits silently, letting me break the thick walls of ice between us.

"He killed her."

Our father straightens his pen more. I want to scream: *Enough with the pen dammit! The pen doesn't need you, I do!* But I don't. I wait. For the strained, civil conversation he preaches.

"I know."

"Why didn't you tell me?"

"He's my client."

"I'm your daughter!" I do scream this time. I scream and I lunge into his office, passing the doorway—the room I'm forbidden from entering. "I'm your daughter! I come first! You tell me if the boy I like killed his girlfriend!"

He raises his voice too, like he has to be heard over a crowded restaurant, not like we're fighting over a life and death situation. "I asked you not to spend time with him."

"That's not enough. That wasn't a real warning. It could have meant anything."

He steeples his fingers. "I said what I could within the confines of the law."

I can't contain my frustration anymore. I don't know if I truly mean what I say, but the words slip out. "I really hate you. Do you know that?"

His mouth falls open a small gap. Enough to hear him gulp down a gust of air.

For once in my life, I see our father falter. He brings his fingers up to grasp the knot of the tie close to his throat. He wiggles it as if it chokes him. "I'm sorry to hear that."

I retreat to my bedroom. Shame and guilt line my stomach, distracting me from previous heartache. I'm frustrated with our father. I have moments where I despise him, but I already regret what I said. I don't hate him. I could never hate anyone.

I don't even hate Dylan.

My brothers join me in my room shortly after I spewed rage at our father. I sit on the bed, knees pulled up to my chest. The sobs have stopped, but my shoulders still shake with silent hiccups.

Conner sits beside me. He presses one of his shoulders against mine in a comforting gesture of solidarity. John sits on the edge of the bed cross-legged.

After a few minutes, Conner nudges me with his shoulder. "Wanna talk about it?"

I shake my head, flinging tears in all directions. "Not about that. We can talk about the others, though."

Conner nods once and John retrieves his little spiral notebook from his front pocket.

"Dylan and Brit were quite the red herring," John says, flipping pages until he ends up on his most recently scrawled list. He draws his pen across the paper. "I'm removing the hiking trail along with Brit's name and timeline from the list."

I wipe tears from my face with the back of my hand. "What do we have left?"

John's monotone recites, "Farmer, pigs, secluded; Ena Jones, Kathy Ray, Jennifer Lowy, unidentified girl times three; Bus stop, fair, barn."

I groan and drop my head back into my lap. "That's not helpful."

"Would you prefer I leave and take my notes with me?"

"No," Conner and I say at the same time.

"They have nothing in common," I say. "Other than age, they're all different. They didn't go to the same school. They didn't hang out with the same people other than Ena and Kathy. They went missing at different times, from different places. Some of them lived in different towns. There's nothing to use. Nothing to go off of. And we know nothing about three of the victims!"

"Maybe the fact that they're all so different is a clue in itself," Conner wonders aloud.

"How so?"

"I think you're onto something," John says, quickly flipping between pages to compare. "They're so different no one would think to connect them. That's what we go off of."

A small headache builds just beneath my brain, above my spine. I close my eyes and focus on the feeling, begging it to leave. The last thing I need today is a headache on top of all the emotional aches sinking into my body. "I feel you're repeating my words back to me in a new order. How is that fact helpful?"

"One sec," Conner says, leaving the room in a hurry.

"Think about it, Delilah," John says. "Someone wanted to make sure these disappearances could never fit together. Never—logically—connect. The bodies were never found, thanks to those disgusting pigs, so everyone assumed the girls ran away, or got themselves lost, or whatever else happens to missing girls."

I squeeze my eyes tighter. I'm still not understanding.

Conner returns and spreads a map of the state across my bed. He's marked red Xs on the locations from my visions, and circled the pig farm.

John gasps which causes Conner and I to gasp in turn. John never gasps. Not ever. He uses his finger to trace along each marking on the map. "They're all in the same county. Only our county."

I notice it now too. The faire is at the southern edge of the border. Emily was abducted near there on her way to meet her friends. She ended up at Octo-tree on the northwest border. Of course, we never found her body, nobody did, but the tree was the same. The pig farm where Ena and Kathy were held sits in the middle of the western section of the county. We found Jennifer's backpack there too.

"It's somebody in the county," John whispers. "Someone wanted to make sure it stayed only within these borders. Why? Who would know the borders?"

"Anyone with a map," Conner says.

"Maybe the killer is an outsider," I suggest, "and wants to keep the crimes in a different county than their own?" The words hold little weight. I've experienced firsthand this killer knows the woods. Someone living miles away would not. Unless they learned for the sole intention of killing girls within those woods.

Conner points at me. "That would make sense. If the police made this connection, they might search for someone here. Not someone out there."

John continues, cycling through information in a quiet voice, only speaking to himself. "What does the county have to do with anything?"

"Or," Conner counters, his pointed finger wilting, "it's a coincidence and doesn't mean anything?"

John's eyes light up as they make contact with mine. "A county official would know the boundaries."

I startle at the sudden eye contact and declaration. "Um, yeah. I guess. So?"

"If they know the boundaries, they know who's doing this, or they're the ones behind it. Are there any county officials with motive, or dubious backgrounds?"

"That's more your expertise than ours." Conner studies the map, running his fingers along the veiny blue and red lines of the roads.

"I care little for politics," John says.

I rush to a crumpled paper ball on my desk, abandoned since my return. I flatten it as I bring it back to my brothers. "The sheriff is running for re-election. He has a brunch event tomorrow morning. I'm sure everyone will be there."

My brothers look up at me. They must wonder the same thing I do. Could the sheriff, the man tasked with keeping us safe, know something he isn't releasing to the public? Could he be protecting someone using this area as a hunting ground?

"That doesn't make sense." I shake my head, but look over the words once more. "If he knew something, he'd stop it. He's the one stuck investigating if someone were to get hurt or go missing."

"Well, he's not trying all that hard," Conner mutters.

"He would know the borders; he would know when the information, the disappearances, affect other police forces," John says. He eyes the invite from across the bed, and I hand it to him. It's not a helpful clue, but I think the act of holding it helps us to think. My brother runs his fingers slowly along the edge of the thick paper. "It doesn't make sense, but what other lead is there?"

The pig farmer, deceased months ago, was our only lead. His son seems innocent. He hasn't been around town long enough to have killed Jennifer, Emily, Ena, or Kathy.

I saw two men. It was never just one. Two men worked together to hurt girls, to dispose of their bodies so we'd never find them. And I still can't figure out the why. Why these girls? Why hurt them at all? Was it fun? Did it emit a rush of adrenaline not found in any other activity?

"What do we do?" Conner asks. His fingers twitch as he waits for his turn to hold the thinking paper. "Do we go to the gala? Do we tell Dad?"

It's not an option, but I'd like to sleep. Forever maybe. Close my eyes and see black and be at peace, with a calm mind, for once.

I sigh, landing on an option that doesn't give me a moment to rest. "We have to go to the gala. We can watch the sheriff, see who he interacts with. I don't know what else to do."

Telling our father is not an option, that is clearer to me than ever before. I'd give him all the information we worked so hard to acquire just for him to throw it in the trash, tell us professionals are on the case, and then send me away again. I can picture his face as he says it. Smug. A smirk pulling his lips from flat to curved. In his mind, he'd be cheering, "I knew it! I knew she wasn't ready."

I'd be isolated again, ripped from my brothers—the only people I care about. The girls would go unavenged for longer, maybe for life. Yeah, no. There is only one option. We have to confront the killer ourselves.

I wake to a soft knock on my bedroom door. I'm surprised to find our father, dressed in a pressed, white button-down and black slacks, standing there. A glance at my alarm clock tells me it's only five in the morning.

"Your brothers and I will be attending brunch. Will you be joining us?"

I sit up and blink sleep from my eyes. We have to go. No one else will keep an eye on the sheriff to find the person he's potentially protecting to ensure another girl isn't killed. "Yeah."

"Be ready by 9:30. I'll be back to pick the three of you up."

He turns and begins to descend the stairs.

"Where are you going?" I ask.

He doesn't slow. "I'm needed at the office. Remember, 9:30."

My brothers and I are ready and waiting on the front porch at 9:30 on the dot—John makes sure of that—but our father is nowhere to be seen.

Conner fiddles with the buttons at the end of his long, white sleeves. "He's late. He's never late."

I yawn loudly. I wasn't able to fall back asleep after the early morning visit from our father. He almost never speaks to me. That's our life since my return—existing without interfering with one another. After my outburst, those awful words I said, I didn't expect an invitation to brunch. I thought I'd have to sneak in, or beg.

And why was he working so early? On a weekday, that wouldn't have caused my thoughts to clash like rusted gears. But as today is Saturday, it's odd. Very odd. Do lawyers have early morning Saturday emergencies? I'd never noticed if he had before.

Conner releases his shoulders from a tense hold, phone in his hand. "Looks like Dad's running late at the office." John stands on his toes to read over Conner's shoulder. "He said he'll meet us there."

We don't question this statement—this change of plans—even though our father isn't the kind of man to 'run late' or move things around. I guess lawyers do have Saturday morning emergencies.

After a drive buzzing with nervous energy, Conner parks his truck beside our father's black car outside town hall.

Our father exits and provides a subtle nod to us. His hair, sleek and styled only just this morning, is frizzy. His shirt seems less pressed somehow, wrinkled and disheveled from constant movement. He doesn't speak, leads us up stone steps instead. I wonder if he's lost in his own mind, or is simply tired of interacting with me.

The event center of town hall hosts the event. Silver and gold balloon arches welcome families from all over town into the large, square room. Blurry shadows reflect off squeaky wood floors as we step inside. Circular tables clothed in white pack the room. A buffet style spread of breakfast foods lines the back wall while a deserted microphone stand waits for its speaker and audience to settle in beside it.

I step off to the side of the entrance, studying as a crowd enters and heads straight for the food. I don't see the sheriff anywhere. As the man of the hour, maybe he'll make a grand entrance followed by a speech. Or maybe he's burying evidence, convincing the whole of Baneberry we don't have a problem with disappearances. The thought forces me to wince. I follow the crowd mingling around the buffet and use a toothpick to set cubed fruit on a little, white paper plate.

I hover at the end of the table where gooey fruit pastries glisten with sugar and glaze. I can't believe these events were once what I looked forward to—where I felt normal. Now, I feel out of place. My white sundress is stiff, itchy, and too tight in the crowded room.

Conner stands among a group of similarly dressed men. He talks with gestating hands, and the group laughs.

I look for John and find him sitting on a metal folding chair tucked into a corner. A hardcover book sits in his lap, and he leans forward to study the words imprinted there.

So much for eyes on the sheriff. It's all up to me now.

Our father stands with a champagne flute filled with orange juice. He's the only adult here not day drinking. Business associates and other professionals in the field of crime solving surround him—I recognize them from the station and courthouse.

I startle when a gruff voice addresses me from behind, on the other side of the pastry table.

"Miss Dufort, have you heard the good news?"

I turn to find Sheriff Barrett watching me. My blood freezes, creating popsicles inside my veins.

He's still in uniform. A paper plate takes up the entirety of his palm. He loads cookies and cupcakes onto the dish until there is no white space left.

I clear my throat. "What good news?"

"The Walker boy turned himself in thanks to you. He didn't say so, but I know you've been spending time together. Nothing inspires a boy to be a man more than a good girl."

I grip the edge of the table, digging my fingertips into a plastic tablecloth. "He turned himself in? When?"

"This morning. As soon as the doors were unlocked to the public." He brings the plate up to his face and bites into the edge of a star-shaped cookie with yellow frosting.

"What did he say?"

The sheriff chews thoughtfully. "That's not something I would normally share with a civilian, but as you were crucial in this, I'll tell you he gave us every detail. There was an altercation. He killed Miss Hill on accident and buried her body in the forest off the trail. Deputies are with him now, checking the burial site. I'm sure it won't take much more convincing to find out where the rest of the missing girls are as well. I thank you for bringing that to my attention."

His words hit me from all angles. Was this his plan all along? Wait for someone—anyone—to commit a violent crime and pin the rest on them? Is this a quick fix, an easy solution to close open cases, to qualify for re-election? It wouldn't be difficult to convince a jury. A small town with no crime, a sudden string of disappearances followed by the admittance to one murder. Our father is good, but not good enough to fight against mob mentality and a secret inside adversary.

Who is the sheriff protecting? And why?

I tread carefully, choosing every word as if poring over a dictionary. "Why—uh—why exactly do you think Dylan killed more than one girl?"

"Who else would have done it?" Barrett barks out a laugh that sends slivers of yellow crumbs across the sweet spread. He saunters over to my side of the table and leans down. "So tell me, Miss Dufort. How'd you do it? How'd you convince him to squeal?"

"I didn't do anything, sir. The guilt must've eaten at him."

He laughs, takes another bite of his cookie, and tucks it into his cheek like a hamster. "Well, you've certainly redeemed yourself, whether or not you had anything to do with Mr. Walker's confession. Consider yourself off my watchlist. You're a good girl after all."

Good girl. *Bad girl.* A shiver races down my spine as those words he kept repeating become clear.

I wait until the sheriff turns to converse with others before I move. My legs advance slowly, fighting a river of invisible snow and ice.

I shove my way through the crowd around Conner. I grab his upper arm and drag him from his conversation to John's chair.

"It's the sheriff," I hiss.

My brothers both stare at Sheriff Barrett with open mouths.

"Don't look at him!"

They turn their heads back to me just as the sheriff looks around to search for a gaze he had to have felt on the back of his head. Our eyes lock. He nods in greeting before resuming his conversation.

"Does he know we're onto him?" Conner asks.

I shake my head, curl fingers around the seams of my dress. "I don't think so."

"How do you know it's him for sure?" John sets a finger on the page of his open book.

"He called me a good girl. In one of my visions, the pig farmer said bad girls get sent to him. And when I saw—was—Ena Jones, she saw a police car right before she was killed. She thought someone reported her missing, that he was there to rescue her. What if he wasn't? What if he was there to kill her? Or he brought her to the pig farm?"

There's still too many frayed threads to keep all the dots from connecting. More gnawed on puzzle pieces. Why would the sheriff work with the pig farmer? Why would the pig farmer kill? Why would the sheriff kill? I look down and realize I'm still holding my paper plate. Four little, orange cubes of cantaloupe bunch together, drawn by the juice coating the surface, cold and soggy against my palm.

Conner holds his hands over his mouth. His eyes are so wide I'm worried they'll stick that way.

Shivers claim my body, buzzing up and down my flesh and leaving behind goosebumps. "He's going to blame Dylan for all the missing girls. He's going to say Dylan hid all their bodies like Brit's."

"How do we prove it was the sheriff?" Conner asks. His gaze darts from my face to just over my shoulder.

I turn to find the sheriff is mimicking Conner's movements, constantly tilting his head to the side to watch us huddled in the corner of his peripherals.

"We can't talk here. He must know I know something."

Conner finds our father to tell him we're heading out as John and I scramble to the truck. Even though it's a warm, sunny day without even a smidgen of shade, my body trembles. This always happens when I'm close to a breakthrough. Adrenaline pumps through my veins faster than my brain can keep up.

John sits beside me on the back bench even though the passenger seat is available if he'd like it. He opens the book on his lap again. His eyes rove across the pages but he never turns to the next one.

When Conner slides into the front seat and turns the keys in the ignition, I lean forward. "We need to go back to the farm."

He wipes an army of sweat building on his hairline. "No way. We have a restraining order, remember? Benjamin might have let it slide once, but twice is a huge risk."

"We need to go somewhere I can trigger a vision. I need to find the missing connection."

"I thought you couldn't trigger visions anymore?" John says.

"I haven't been able to, but I need to try. I need to find this missing piece, or we'll never have enough to turn him in."

"What happens when the sheriff follows us? Kills us on an isolated pig farm with no one around to hear our screams?"

Conner shudders and his face pales. He doesn't move to wrap his hands around the steering wheel.

"He won't follow us," I say as more people enter the building. "Everyone came to see him. He won't be able to get away until the event is over."

Conner and John share a look.

"You're positive?" Conner asks, "absolutely positive that the only way we solve this is at the farm?"

It has to be the pig farm. It's where the girls ended up, well, most of them. There's a connection there we can't figure out yet, but we have to try.

"Yes. I am."

Conner carefully directs the truck down a shallow ditch so it can't be seen from the highway.

Instead of stepping foot in the meadow, we stick to the tree line, hidden behind tall, thick trunks.

When we reach the side of the house, I stop, holding up my hand. The air feels different from when I was last here with Dylan—heavy with weeping secrets begging to be discovered. I listen for any sound or sign of Ben and the pigs. All I hear is the call and communication of chirping birds shuffling through tree branches.

We sneak up to the farmhouse porch. The house looks dusty and decrepit still. Uninhabitable. A shredded railing lies in the grass, tangled among overgrown greenery, decorated with thick white webbing and dotted with spiders. Shards of wood still line the porch, splintered fingers uselessly reaching for their remains.

I knock on the front door. Hollow echoes ring out. My ear hovers beside the weathered wood, searching for footsteps throughout the house. There are none.

"Do you think he left already?" Conner asks. I shrug. The white trailer loaded with pigs is gone, but the truck remains, parked alongside the barn. He could still be here.

I knock with less confidence this time. Benjamin Simms doesn't seem to be coming. I cannot tell if this is good or bad.

Conner shuffles weight back and forth on each leg. John looks around at the molding, fuzzy wooden planks of the house's exterior. He measures tufts of grass growing up from beneath the porch steps by placing his shoe next to them. "Does he even live here?"

"He did a few days ago." I knock again. The sound is weak and pitiful—a whispered echo.

"What now?" Conner snaps his fingers silently and rolls his shoulders.

I grip the flaking golden door knob.

"Veto," John says before I can even turn it.

"He's clearly not here right now," I say, hand still gripping the knob. "We need to go inside. It's the only way. He won't tell on us."

"He will if we break in a second time," John says.

"Can you keep watch then?"

John sighs, but doesn't object.

Conner and I step inside the house while John waits in the open doorway, his back to us. Furniture covers nearly every inch of space. Thick layers of dust carpet the floor. Clear shoe prints paint a path in three directions: left, right, and up a set of narrow stairs flanked by wood-slatted walls.

"This looks just like the *Texas Chainsaw Massacre* house," Conner whispers, raising his eyebrows at me.

I peer into each room. A kitchen and dining room on the right. A sitting room on the left. Possibly bedrooms upstairs. "I guess we take a little tour until we see something. Or trigger something."

Conner decides on the kitchen first. He steps into the shoe prints left behind. Dust stirs with each movement.

I stand at the most middle point of the room as I can, squeezing my body in between a countertop decorated with grime and a dining table stacked with stained plates and crusty silverware.

I close my eyes and listen to the sounds of the house. The groaning of the foundation as gusts of wind slip through open windows. The distant scrabbling of some sort of rodent or critter nesting in the walls. I will a vision to take over. To guide me.

It feels wrong, wishing to see another person die, but it could save more from the same horrible end and bring justice to those already gone.

I open my eyes when a rattle pierces my thoughts like broken glass. Conner stands before the fridge, one hand atop the open door while he leans to look into it.

"Hungry already?"

"Not for any of this. Take a look."

Images of severed body parts pickled in jars spring to my mind. Thankfully, that's not what I find. Instead, the fridge is full of food long rotted into inedible mush. Little black balls that may have once been oranges. A plastic-wrapped loaf of green bread. Two blackened bananas still bunched together. The smell only reaches my nose after I realize what I'm looking at.

Conner slams the fridge closed. "Alright, so Benjamin Simms doesn't live here."

We follow the footprints back to the entrance, then to the sitting room. They don't make it far into the space, stopping in front of a ratty fabric couch. Yellow-edged newspapers pile on cushions. I scan the articles and dates on top. The most recent is from a year ago, but it's nothing special—the announcement of a new building in town.

"This is all his father's stuff," I say. "He must have left everything invaluable behind. Including the food."

Conner and I sift through the newspapers. Maybe the man that once lived here kept records of the girls he killed—proof of notoriety.

"What was Benjamin like?" Conner asks.

"He didn't defend his father. Only said *he'd* never kept any girls in the barn."

"Do you think he was hiding something?"

"I don't know. Maybe? He wasn't secretive. More...sad. Regretful."

Conner stops searching through the papers to stand and stretch. "Sounds like a side effect of guilt to me."

"Could be." I finish looking through the papers too. Not many of the girls ended up in the news, but the ones that did aren't here. Those particular articles could be stashed somewhere else. Or nowhere at all.

We return to the entrance to check on John. Benjamin couldn't have left town. Not with his truck parked in the field. When John informs us he has nothing to report, we make our way up the stairs.

Conner goes first, placing his feet in prints marring the dust. He stops halfway up. "Hmm."

"What? What's wrong?"

"There's two sets of footprints on the stairs."

I look down. Conner is right, but I don't find this as bizarre as he does. "Benjamin probably took a few trips to get everything he needed, that's all."

Conner shakes his head. "Not unless he changed shoes in between trips." He points to a pair on the left, pressed against the wall. It almost looks like the walker was sneaking up the stairway. "The back is curved, see? And the tips are pointed. Those are cowboy boots." He points to the right, the steps we've adopted. "These are sneakers."

I lower my voice. "I know someone who wears cowboy boots."

"Me too." Conner holds a finger to his lips. He creeps up the stairs like a cartoon character, stepping with only the toes of his shoes.

Doors line the hallway at the top floor. Without a discussion or a look, my brother and I both head to the one at the very end where the door stands ajar.

The room is dark. Newspapers plaster the windows. Only a brown glow lies on the other side.

Conner slips one arm inside to flip on the light switch. A single bulb hanging in the middle of the room hums on.

A wooden bed frame with ceiling-high columns on each end sits in the middle of the room. Several handmade quilts make up the bed. A layer of dust on the top quilt is almost a blanket itself in thickness. Benjamin Simms clearly did not sleep here.

The footprints in this room become a jumbled mess on the floor. Dust climbs the baseboards of the walls.

Conner grabs my arm with a yelp.

I follow his gaze.

Half a leg lies on the floor on the other side of the bed.

Together, we slowly circle the edge of the room.

The leg turns into two legs. Then a torso. Then a head.

Benjamin Simms lies face-up. His eyes and mouth are both wide open. His pallor has already taken on the greasy, bloodless sheen of the dead.

My breath catches in my throat, lodged like a foreign object.

I've never seen a corpse before. I've *seen* them in visions, but it's completely different being in my own body, using Delilah eyes to witness this.

He doesn't smell yet. If anything, I think I may smell human waste. But the rotting smell of a forgotten corpse doesn't rise from the body yet. He was killed recently.

A small wound, the size of a shirt button, lines up with his heart in the middle of his chest.

"He—uh. He—" I clear my throat. "He was shot. I think."

Conner nods mutely, still gripping my arm.

"We should probably leave," I whisper. I'm not stupid. My brothers and I will not wait around a fresh dead body for a vision. There are some things I have to let the police handle. Maybe if we report this, the deputies will arrive before the sheriff. He won't be able to twist the story, dispose of the body. This could be what gets him caught.

Conner swallows. "I think that's a good idea." He leaves, stirring up dust to settle on Benjamin's legs.

In the doorway, I turn back to look at the body once more.

It's no longer there.

Thick dust tops the empty space.

"Hello. Hello."

I creep into the hallway leading to the stairs. The front door swings closed behind Sheriff Barrett.

"Oh, hello." The voice that leaves my lips is deep. A man's. It is Benjamin Simms' voice.

The sheriff starts up the stairs. His age shows as he clings to the bannister with both hands and leans against the wall. Why is this man running for re-election? He's clearly ready to retire.

Halfway up, Barrett stops. "I was told you wanted to speak with me." He takes a deep breath. "Something about pigs and a barn."

I step deeper into the hallway to be heard. "Yes, but I made an appointment to speak with you tomorrow. In your office."

The sheriff reaches the top of the stairs. He waves my statement off. "I was in the area. Figured I'd save you the trip."

He moves closer. His breath smells like campfire smoke. It reminds me of pig slop. "So, whatcha got for me?" He places his hands on his hips—his fingers only inches away from a holstered gun.

"Nothing much. Only a few questions."

I lead him to the back bedroom. Disgust creeps up my throat. Memories of screams, blood, and violence paint the wallpapered walls.

"I was looking for my mom's good jewelry." We stop in front of the dresser. My fingers tremble as I open the top drawer. "I found some...unsightly...things instead."

I step back, allowing the sheriff to make his own conclusions. I suck in a breath when he reaches into the drawer without gloves to pull out an orange bottlecap necklace. He holds it up to the covered windows, twisting it every which way to scrutinize with the aid of a muted rising sun.

He drops the necklace to inspect more objects. Three small, golden hoop earrings crusted with what I hope isn't blood. A pair of black-framed, oval glasses, one lens cracked. A tube of lipstick. The sheriff pops the top of the tube off, revealing a bright pink tint.

"Well, that sure is an odd collection." He drops the lipstick back into the drawer. It bounces once then sticks to one of the golden earrings. "Not to speak ill of the dead, but your Pa might have been interested in things you weren't privy to."

"No—that's not—"

"Well then, these must have belonged to your mother."

I shake my head. "There's no way. What if these are," I lean in close to whisper, as if my deceased father is across the room listening in, "what if these are trophies?"

He laughs. The sound is a boom. A clap of thunder. "For what sport, boy?"

I keep my voice a whisper. It feels safer that way. "Trophies from kills."

The sheriff leans back to stare at me with squinted eyes.

"Like a hunter collecting antlers," I explain.

"I know what a trophy is. What I don't know is why you'd think your father was a killer."

I stop myself from shaking my head again, and tilt it to the side instead. "I don't, really. It's just—see these kids came around yesterday. They put some nasty thoughts in my head."

Barrett presses his lips together. His fingers fiddle with his belt, pulling at the buckle.

"And I found some weird things around the house, in the barn—"

"What kind of weird things?"

I gesture to the still-open drawer. "This. And some pictures."

"I need to see those pictures."

The sheriff's fingers twitch, jumping from his belt buckle to his holster. The movement turns my spine to ice.

"Sure thing." I make slow movements. Something has set him off, alarmed him. He can't think these trophies are mine, can he?

I lead him to the other side of the bed where an end table hides.

I open the drawer. Empty other than a messy stack of polaroids. I only looked at about six on top before it made me sick and I stopped at the sheriff's office to schedule an appointment.

He pushes past me to access the drawer. He pins my body against his hard holster and the wall. Scooping the polaroids up, he flips through them, dropping them back into the drawer as he looks.

I watch each one as it drops. Pictures of young girls—teenagers, some of them barely older than children—sit or lay in the barn. Some battered and bruised. Others bloody. All look asleep. I pray to heaven above they're asleep.

The sheriff's features shift. His cool, unworried demeanor disappears, falling off his face in an instant. I shrink back against the wall when he turns to me. "How many of these did you look at?"

I lie. I can't help it. It's a survival instinct I picked up as a child. I only looked at a few of the pictures, skimmed them mostly, but the sheriff is angry. These pictures can be the difference between walking away or a beating. "None. I mean, I saw the one on top, but I didn't really look at it. I think I saw blood and panicked. I called you immediately. I didn't look at anything else."

The sheriff laughs again. A thunderous sound. It sounds far too similar to my late father's laugh. Mocking. Without joy. Deceitful. "You really thought you could blackmail me? Me!"

I shake my head so ferociously the room tilts to one side. "No, of course not. Blackmail you for what? My father was the bad guy here clearly. Nobody else."

Barrett holds a picture up to my face so close the image is a blur of black and white. "You think I'm dumb?"

The photo clears. My stomach disappears like the sheriff's smile, choosing a new poor sucker to sit in.

He holds a body. Sheriff Barrett holds a body. A young girl with ratty blonde hair. Ripped jeans. A black t-shirt. He clearly didn't know this picture was being taken. He emerges from trees, a path I have not seen on the property. He cranes his neck to peer behind, ensuring no one has followed. His arms sag from the weight of her—level with his upper thighs. My jaw hangs open. Words no longer exist.

"Who did you tell about this picture?"

My tongue flails in my mouth, searching for words. Begging for words. For anything to say to defend myself.

The sheriff drops the photo back into the drawer. He pulls his gun out and presses it against my chest. "Who did you tell about this picture? Did you tell those kids?"

"No—nobody. I never saw that picture, I swear."

He doesn't lower the gun, but collects the pile of photographs with his free hand. "I'll be confiscating these."

"Of course," I say. My tongue is a raisin, shriveled into nearly nothing. "Take whatever you need. You know I'm leaving town today, right? You won't have to deal with me again. You'll never see my face. I'll be like a ghost."

The sheriff sighs. He backs up, his gun no longer pressing against my sternum. I free my spine from its prison against the wall. "I'd like to believe you. I really would."

I bring my hands together. "Believe me. I'm sure whatever you and my father were working on was important. Reasonable. I would never want to get in the way of a sheriff's duties to his town."

The sheriff doesn't argue. Doesn't explain. He pulls the trigger.

The bullet tears through my body. Punching bone shards deep inside my chest where they scatter among blood, tissue, sinew.

The jolt sends me to the floor.

Barrett scoops up the odd assortment of trophies from the drawer before he leaves. As his footsteps drag down the stairs, I want to call for him, beg him to stay. I don't want to be abandoned in this room again. Even if he's the one who did this to me.

Alone, darkness steals my vision.

I'm being dragged roughly down the stairs when the vision clears. I almost tumble down the last several steps and have to cling to the banister to keep my footing.

"Don't hurt her!" Conner's voice is coated in anger, but his words wobble.

I blink up at the man apprehending me. It's exactly who I expected. Cowboy boots shuffle down the steps beside me. A holstered gun presses against my hip bone.

We round the corner where my brothers are handcuffed together, sitting on the floor, backs against the couch.

They struggled while I was trapped in Benjamin Simms' last moments. Newspapers no longer only pile atop the couch. They scatter, crumpled and ripped, across the entire room.

The sheriff throws me to the floor beside John who has entered a paralyzed state of panic.

Sheriff Barrett paces. His head is down, but he doesn't regard the newspapers. Each step crinkles like a miniature crack of lightning.

Conner clears his throat. His voice is hoarse. He must have been screaming long before I heard anything. "You can let us go. You don't have to do this. We won't say a thing."

The sheriff snorts. "You think I haven't heard that before?"

I open my mouth. The words are faster than my brain. "If you gave anyone a chance to prove themselves—"

Conner leans in front of John to set me with a death stare. This is his operation. He's been handling things for several minutes now. I clamp my mouth shut.

"What my sister means is you should give us a chance. We'll keep our word."

The sheriff stops. His boots land on an article about a fire that burned down a bakery five years ago and claimed two lives. I remember investigating that with our father. We thought it was arson. "Do you hear yourself, Mr. Dufort? You're asking me to let you go. Three of you."

Conner nods. "Yes, exactly. The three of us won't say a thing."

"Three versus one," Barrett waves his gun above his head. A wild, crazed gesture. "If you talk, there are three of you. Nobody is going to think three of you lied or made up this experience."

"It would never get that far," Conner pleads. "We won't say anything. We'll forget all about it."

"Will you now?" The sheriff lowers his gun to rest against his thigh. His eyes are a scanner, sending a beam of analysis across the three of us. He moves toward us, and I flinch. He grabs John by the collar. "What about this one? He doesn't seem capable of forgetting."

The muscles in Conner's arms flex. Still, he restrains himself from an ambush. "John isn't a problem. He'll do what you ask."

"Is that true, John?" The sheriff leans in close. Too close. Even I can see the red lines running across the whites of his eyes, blue veins bulging from his forehead, sweat building on his upper lip, a slight tremor in his chin.

I'm afraid John won't answer. I'm afraid the sheriff will take his frustration out on my sweet, innocent brother. But after a moment, John swallows. Probably to clear the lump in his throat that Conner and I also choke on. "Yes, sir."

The sheriff releases John's collar. "He speaks!"

John returns to his still shell. I watch as a film—a lens—covers his eyes, taking his gaze from present to elsewhere. Taking his brain, his responses with it, to a safer place far from here. Back in his bedroom, I imagine. Reading a book about the history of the railway, or all the sea creatures hidden in the dark depths of the ocean.

Conner continues to plead with the pacing sheriff, and I think. My older brother is trying his best, I know he is, but his words won't be what gets us out of this situation. We need action. We need to move. We need to get out of this house. Off this farm. This is a place of death, and we're moving closer to that end with each word.

I think back to my visions. The sheriff was never in any of them. No—wait. That's not true. He was in one. In the car. He was the man that gave a ride to Emily. He shot her under octo-tree. But why her? Why kill her but not the rest? The rest died here. Bludgeoned and bloody. Why was her death clean and quick in comparison?

As she died...what did she hear? Footsteps. She heard footsteps. She thought it was her friends, but her body was never found. She was never even reported missing. At least, not that my brothers and I could find when we researched her later. I still don't know her full name.

Her body was moved.

A wave of cold washes over me as if I'm a corpse left among the trees. Her body was moved. *She was disposed of.* The same as the rest. They were all disposed of here. They must have been. But why? Why team up? Why kill at all? Why? Why? Why?

I look up only when silence takes over crunching pacing and endless pleading. The silence almost hurts. It's the sound right before a gunshot.

Conner has given up, or is thinking of something new to say— something to make this man change his mind.

The sheriff closes his eyes. His chest heaves. Tears escape his eyelids.

No. No. No. No. No.

He's decided.

He knows what he must do.

"I'm sorry. I don't want to do this—not to good kids—but I have to protect myself." He lifts the gun. He points it at Conner first. Aimed at his chest. His heart. His strong, healthy, beating heart full of empathy and love and understanding.

I can't catch my breath. I can't lose my brothers. I need them.

"Wait—wait!"

The sheriff's eyes cut to me.

"What if—what if we were accomplices? Then we can't tell. We'd get in trouble too."

He doesn't lower the gun. It looks at Conner's still beating heart. Coveting it. Wishing to tear through it.

"You came back for the body, right?" I continue. I must have his attention. Or else my world would be shattered by now. "What if we—we help you get rid of the body? The pigs are gone, aren't they? You need to get rid of the body a new way. A better way. No trace?"

The sheriff lowers the gun inch by painstakingly slow inch—until it's pointed at the floor.

"John is a genius. He could whip up something. A liquid to—to dissolve the body." I'm not practiced in lying, and words only come to my mind along with each beat of my heart. I can only hope he doesn't see through me. He's a sheriff trained with liars and criminals, but he's clearly not thinking straight. He's just as much a mess as me and my brothers.

"Is it true?" he barks at John whose whole body startles. "Can you do that?"

I look at John and nod slowly. He isn't a liar either. None of us are. But we have to try. We need time. We need the gun pointed at the floor, away from Conner's chest, long enough to get out of here.

John swallows again. He is barely audible when he says, "Yes. I can. I can create an acid to dissolve the body."

"What will you need?"

"A tarp," I say first, stalling for John to think of something. I wouldn't be surprised if he knew the chemical components required to dissolve a human corpse. He is the smartest person I know, after all. But thinking of that on a whim, with a deranged, gun-toting killer, cannot be easy.

"A bone saw," Conner says next. "To cut it up. It's easier to dissolve small pieces."

"A tub of some sort," I add. We're listing everything but the actual chemicals. I hope John has that part covered soon.

The sheriff holsters his gun. The three of us breathe out in relief.

"Lye," John says.

"Lye?" The sheriff crosses his arms and raises his eyebrows.

"Yes, lye. Like in soap. I'll need a lot. Several gallons. The hardware store should have some, though, not in that quantity."

"Miss Dufort," the sheriff says. "Will you be able to locate this lye without your brother present?"

"She can read a label," John assures. However, it's not that assuring. I don't want to be separated. I don't want to be alone. I don't want my brothers out of my sight for a single second.

Sheriff Barrett locks my brothers up in the barn. They're still handcuffed together, sitting against the back wall.

I watch from the backseat of the sheriff's car as he loops chains around the barn doors, securing them again, and ensuring I obey. There's no way my brothers can get out of this. Conner and John could try pulling the door off its hinges again, but I doubt that would work. John isn't the exercising type, and Conner needed Dylan's help last time.

That means the rest is up to me. I need a plan. Something to say or do to get us out of this new predicament. I squirm in place, buckled up exactly where Emily sat however long ago—a girl who died minutes after taking this seat.

The window to my right is new. The other windows are sun-stained, old and brown at the edges, while this one is clear as water.

We drive in silence. The only sound the low hum of a moving vehicle over a rough road. I hope my brothers are having more luck coming up with some kind of plan to get us out of this. There's not much

I can do on my end. Except maybe scream for help when we reach the hardware store, but that's a quick and easy way to get Conner and John killed. The sheriff would have a head start back to the pig farm. A vehicle. A gun, loaded with bullets pining for my older brother's heart.

I startle in my seat when the sheriff breaks the silence. "It wasn't supposed to get so messy. I had it all planned out."

I meet his eyes through the rearview mirror. Will this save us? Being his listening ear, his confidant? "What happened?" I'm not sure what part of his killings I'm referring to, but it gets him talking.

"Small towns with small minds. They thought I wasn't good enough for re-election. Doesn't matter there's almost no crime in my jurisdiction. There were teenagers who smoked pot, and drank, and ran around during late hours of the night."

Words I heard before, from the sheriff and the pig farmer, echo in my head: *bad girls.*

"Had to get rid of 'em. It was the only way. Nobody could see how clean this place really was until there were no more degenerates loitering about."

My stomach roils. These girls were not bad. They were not degenerate. They did what they could to find amusement in a place with nothing. They tried new experiences. They lived, and they died for it.

"The bad girls had to go. They just had to."

I bite down on a retort. He needs to think I'm one of the good ones.

"Wasn't even hard, truthfully. Most of the parents were easy enough to convince. Their kid was already hardly ever home. Easy to assume she found a new home. The real troublemakers didn't even have parents that cared. They had money troubles. Marriage troubles. Career troubles. At least their primary trouble was gone."

The urge to wrap my hands around his throat rises up my arms painfully. My blood burns, alight with disgust. I breathe deeply through my nose until I can speak without crying. "Why only girls? What about bad boys?"

The sheriff cocks his head to the side, watching me through the mirror as we enter the hardware store's parking lot. He presses his lips together and lets out a gentle hum. "Because there are no bad boys."

A flood of white coats my eyes. I want to scream. I want to kick and hit and bite and scratch and claw. I want Conner to hold this man's arms behind his back as John and I take turns hurting him.

Sheriff Barrett exits the vehicle and walks around to my side. I huff air into my nose so quickly it sounds like I'm stuffed up.

Is this how our father felt whenever he finished an investigation and confronted the murderer—full of disgust and rage? Did he want to kill the killer? If I could, would I kill the sheriff? I think I would. He doesn't deserve prison time. A trial. A chance to argue and blame girls who aren't here to defend themselves. He deserves pain. He deserves to suffer. He deserves death.

He opens the door to release me, cupping his hand over my head to make sure I don't bump it against the roof. The action makes me angrier.

He smiles and nods to everybody we pass through the store on our way to where the lye should be. My gaze meets each pair of eyes I see, urging them to ask questions, realize something is amiss. Nobody notices.

I find a bottle immediately, among drain cleaners. It's on the bottom shelf, almost sitting on the floor. It's small, the size of a mayonnaise jar, and filled with powder. We would need a lot of bottles, more than the store has stocked.

We purchase every unit available, and the remaining three stored in the back.

Nobody asks questions. Nobody wonders why the sheriff purchases a suspicious amount of lye, why the Dufort girl follows. It's suddenly obvious to me why so many girls went missing—unreported and unsearched for—for so long. This town is oblivious. They don't care. They don't question. Baneberry residents live in their small town bubble, happy as long as their days are happy, blind to the turmoil of others' around them.

The sheriff locks me in the backseat of the car while he loads paper bags filled with lye in the trunk. "We'll have to make do with what we got," he says when he slides behind the wheel.

When we reach the barn, the sheriff drags me from the car before unloading the chemicals, dropping containers on the ground atop a dusty patch of dirt. He keeps one hand wrapped around my wrist while the other fiddles with the locks. "I'm going to open the door now," he says, dropping the padlock and unwrapping chains from handles. "Stay back against the wall, boys. If you try anything, it's Miss Dufort who will suffer the consequences."

Do the cowboy boots mean he's fast like in those western movies Conner loves? Will he unholster his weapon faster than I can rip my arm from his grasp, hop the fence, and take cover?

He throws open one of the barn doors and wrenches my arm, positioning me in front of him like a shield.

I blink through the darkness.

The boys are not here.

The sheriff notices at the same time I do. His grip tightens. He presses his weapon against my back. It digs into my spine as he shoves me forward. "Get out where I can see you. Now!"

Silence.

The barn is so quiet it hurts. Stillness plugs my ears, digging like parasites to find my brain.

He shoves me deeper into the darkness.

My brothers didn't leave discernable tracks. If anything, they ran around, kicking aside dirt, straw, and dust to create a path so chaotic, it can't be tracked and followed.

The sheriff shoves me forward again, into the dark hallway between stalls. "I'm not asking. Get out where I can see you!" His hand trembles, dragging steel up and down my spine.

Sweat builds along my hairline. The air is stagnant, suffocating. I hope my brothers got out. If they didn't, if they're hiding within the shadows in the stalls, they're going to be shot. I feel it. An electric tingle in the tips of my fingers. The sheriff is done with our game, our negotiation. He will kill all three of us.

Our father might be as easily swayed as the other parents. After all, he'd be rid of three burdens. He'd have a big, empty house all to himself. He could start over. Find a wife. Have children, moldable ones from scratch. Not scared and traumatized eight-year-olds suspicious of everyone around them.

The sheriff kicks open the stall nearest to us, the one with a grotesque sheet bundled in a corner. The metal gate swings inward with a scream. The barn shudders when it thumps against the wooden wall.

He yanks me to the next stall.

He kicks a wailing gate in again.

Empty.

The gun digs into my spine until it scratches against my bones, grinds against vertebrae. He uses his other hand to grip the back of my neck, fingers imbedding bruises, and directs me to the next stall. His palms are slick with sweat, but cold. My time may run out soon. His impatience grows, strangled, huffing breaths against my hair, as his boots kick in each stall.

Empty.

Empty.

Empty.

"You have until the count of ten! Or Miss Dufort dies. Do I make myself clear?"

He shoves me to the ground. Do I look at him as he murders me? Do I watch in adrenaline-fused slow motion as a bullet careens into my heart?

No, I've seen enough death. I'd like mine to be as peaceful as possible. I won't watch. I'll stare at the slats of a barn wall when he kills me.

Except, he doesn't kill me. Nor does he count to ten. Instead, he grunts and shuffles his boots around.

I turn and press my back against the wall.

Conner and Sheriff Barrett fight over the gun, stuck in between both palms. John crouches at the end of the hall, holding himself with shaking arms.

A pop rings out. I scream. The gun falls. Conner kicks it to John who grabs it with the tips of his fingers and tucks it into his suit jacket.

The sheriff stumbles, but he doesn't bleed. He leans against the small space in between open metal gates and sighs.

"Don't move," Conner growls. He helps me stand. Tears fill my eyes as my hands search for a wound to plug, a place to put pressure, along his arms and torso. "I'm okay, Lilah. It hit the ceiling. We're all okay."

We couldn't have been that lucky, could we? We must be. Conner is dry, not a drop of blood on him. Only cold, sticky sweat.

Our father rushes into the barn. He's lost his suit jacket somewhere between the gala and here. He assesses everyone strewn around the room. "Is anyone injured?"

John's trembling arms retrieve the gun and hand it to our father. He clicks the safety on before stuffing it between the waist of his pants and his tucked in button-down.

"What are you doing here? When did you get here?" I gulp stale air. The shock helps to clear my tears.

"Did you know Dad can pick locks?" Conner beams at our father.

"What?"

Our father moves to me next, checking me like I did to Conner only a moment ago. "Are you alright?" My stare settles on his. He's never asked me that before, and I don't know how to respond. Physically, yes. But any other sense of the word? No. Not at all.

"I said, did you know—"

"—I got that part," I interject. "What are you doing here? When?"

When our father is satisfied with his perusal of my lack of injuries, he focuses on the sheriff, still huffing against the wall. Benjamin Simms was right. This man needs to retire. Now, he can do so in prison.

"John takes excellent notes," our father says. He crouches beside the sheriff. Somehow, his shining black shoes still haven't picked up a speck of dust. It feels like the most absurd part of the day.

"Barrett, why?"

"You're no idiot, Nathaniel. You know why. Town's full of ingrates." The sheriff struggles to regain his breath. His altercation with Conner has damaged him. Hopefully irreparably.

"Why Elias?"

Elias? Is that the pig farmer? Benjamin Simms' father?

The sheriff's breathing steadies. "We had an arrangement."

"Blackmail?"

How had I never noticed before? Our father is incredibly good at this. I mean, obviously. I've worked with him before, and we had a great solve record. But I never realized just how good he is. I never would have thought blackmail. I never would have made any of these conclusions. I hadn't even figured out the pig farmer's name yet. Maybe in another week I could have had it. Maybe...

"Nobody disappears around here without me knowing. It's my job." The sheriff coughs. It makes me and John jump. Both of us still feel the sound of the gunshot pinging around our eardrums. We've always been sensitive to sound. Conner wraps an arm around my shoulder in a side hug.

Barrett laughs. "'She fell into the pen. Eaten by the pigs while my boy and I slept soundly.' What a load of hooey."

"In exchange for not turning him in..." I mutter. The puzzle pieces fit together, creating a hideous, bloody picture. "You had him feed your other victims to the pigs. Innocent girls."

"Bad girls."

I clench my jaw at his correction, my teeth grinding against one another. Why does this man get to live? How many girls died at his hand? I only know of a few, a handful. There could be many more.

Unnamed, never getting their true justice. And there's nothing I can do about it.

Sirens lament, shrieking through the trees to the barn and my shocked and reeling mind. In no longer than a breath, deputies swarm the building, beige uniforms and drawn steel.

"Conner," our father says, loudly, over scuffling feet and barking orders. His gaze does the rest of the talking as it flicks from John to me.

Conner guides me from the barn, sweeping John up in his other arm as we exit. Several cars circle the building, grills pressed against the worn wood fence. Red and blue lights twist, colors bouncing off the barn, Benjamin Simms' house, and rows and rows of watching trees.

I don't pay attention to where we're going until Conner stops walking, tightening his grip around my back to stop me too. We're at the edge of the meadow, looking into the darkness where tree trunks and roots cluster.

I don't know how Conner manages to lead John and I with a level head, clear and concise in his instruction. It must be his leadership instincts kicking in during a crisis. He's always been good at that—he gets it from our father. John and I turn mechanical, we short circuit, cease to speak, function. We got that from our mother.

The three of us sit with our backs to the forest. The cool breath of the trees grazes my skin, drying sweat until my dress no longer clings so tight to my body. My legs tremble, little electrical currents shooting from my toes to my thighs. The shock of today's events hits John harder. His teeth chatter, clacking together at a speed almost comparable to hummingbird wings. Conner squeezes us both against him, stuck being the strong one again.

Our father and one deputy emerge from the barn with Sheriff Barrett in tow, handcuffs securing his hands behind his back. They plant Barrett in the back of a cruiser.

"How?" The single word is all I can accomplish.

"He showed up right after you and the sheriff left," Conner says. We watch as our father hands the confiscated gun over to the lone deputy.

"The sheriff left the gala right after we did," Conner continues. "He didn't announce it or anything, just slipped out the doors after making sure nobody was watching him."

More deputies trickle out of the barn. Some head for the house. Others retrieve cameras and begin taking pictures of the barn, the pigpen, the empty trough.

"Dad looked over John's notes some more, figured out what was going on, and got here right as we were being locked in the barn. He picked the lock on the door, and on our cuffs—that was cool. Then we told him everything."

One of the deputies runs from the house. He yells something I can't hear from this distance, and the others follow him into the building, cameras and a black bag in hand.

"He was in the middle of calling the station when you and the sheriff came back. Dad wanted us to stay hidden while he went to get you, but we couldn't just sit around while a murderer held a gun to your back, so I charged in."

I look at Conner as he ducks his head, a sheepish blush turning his cheeks pink. He disobeyed, acted on his own, for me. Like old times.

John clears his throat before whispering. "We couldn't leave you alone in there with him, and help was taking too long."

The deputies talk to Conner first, then John, then me, writing our statements and nodding along with each word. Of course, they ask why in the world three high-schoolers on summer break cared to investigate old disappearances. We give vague answers, a mix of 'fueled by curiosity' and 'we thought this had something to do with Brit.'

When we're told we're free to go back home, our father walks my brothers and I to Conner's truck. None of us speak, too tired to form words, expel any more statements.

Our father's car is parked nearby, tucked into bushes at the side of the road. The black sheen is gone, covered with stray leaves and sticks, dusty from the unpaved road.

The drive home is silent as well. Conner even turns the volume knob on the stereo down, silencing jovial guitar string plucking and lyrics about summer nights and fireflies. I turn to watch out the wide back window as our father follows, driving as close to the truck as he can. When our eyes meet, he looks away, studying his mirrors.

I still can't believe it—the events following the sheriff's re-election gala. A case I've been working for over a week, with the help of my brothers, our father solved in an hour.

I'm in the conference room again, but this time Dylan sits across from me. He's changed into a gray sweatsuit.

"Thank you for visiting me," he says with a shy smile. His hair looks like he tried to comb it with his fingers as it lays flat and frizzy against his scalp.

"I didn't come for you. I came for answers."

His smile drops.

"I need to know why you dragged me into this," I say.

He tilts his head to the side. "Into what?"

"Into your case. You killed Brit. Why did you want me to solve it? You could have gotten away with it if you hadn't brought me in. The police were onto you, but they had nothing. You threw away your chances for what reason?"

"Maybe that's why."

I throw up my hands. When they come back down, my palms slap against the table harder than expected. Dylan and I both startle in our seats. "You wasted my time, nearly sabotaged another case, because you wanted to get caught?"

Dylan shakes his head with that shy smile again. "I didn't want to get caught."

I stand. I need to lie down. Take a nap after all that's happened since my return. These disappearances and murders nearly put me in another hospital, and I've only had one night of sleep since the sheriff's attack and arrest yesterday.

"Just listen," Dylan whispers. He rests his hands on the table. Metal cuffs hold his wrists close together.

When I don't sit back down, but don't leave the room either, Dylan continues, "I didn't feel a single thing after I—after what happened between me and Brit on that trail."

I slowly lower myself back into the seat.

"You can't even imagine how awful that feels," he says. "I hurt my girlfriend, the only girl I've ever loved. She's gone from the world forever because of me. And I didn't feel a thing."

Even though anger coats my heart like a candy shell, a small crack of empathy carves across the surface. Not empathy for what Dylan did, of course not. Empathy for his regret. For the understanding he didn't work and feel the same way other people did. Empathy for his difference. If anyone understands, I do.

"Police, detectives, my dad—they all interviewed me. I didn't look guilty because I didn't *feel* guilty. It was just another day, but one without Brit, and I didn't mind one bit." He squeezes his hands together, interlocking fingers.

"And then one day, I woke up, and I couldn't take it anymore. I wanted to feel something. A life, an important life, was gone from the world and I wanted to care." He twists his fingers as they're still interlocked. I grimace and focus on his face.

A line of tears falls down Dylan's cheek now. "I realized that I wasn't just numb to Brit's death—I was numb to everything. Hurting her hurt me, you know? I was alive, but I didn't feel alive. I felt cold, gray. Like a body with nothing left inside of it."

"And then I just missed her so much." Dylan sobs now, dropping his head into his chained hands. I look away, granting him the kindness of letting him sob himself dry without judgemental eyes.

He wipes his nose across the sleeve of his sweatshirt. "I knew you helped your father before. He mentioned it once. Said you were coming home so he wouldn't be available for counsel on a certain date. At first, I wanted to make sure you wouldn't find anything. That I covered it up so well, not even some girl with intuition or visions or whatever you have could figure out what really happened. But after spending so much time with you—"

Dylan points to the left of the table at a box of tissues. I slide them closer to him. He blows his nose and blots his eyes. This moment is certainly not one of victory, but I feel a smidgen of pride on behalf of Brit.

Dylan clears his throat and looks at me. "I started to like you too, Delilah. Honestly. Truly. I did."

I don't have a response for that. What does one say when a killer admits to liking them?

"As I watched you work and interact with your brothers, the numbness went away and the guilt came. How could I have done...that...to Brit? I could never think of harming you, of taking you from the world, from your family. So how had I already done it?" He shakes his head and trades a crumpled tissue between each hand.

"I'll never forgive myself. The guilt will never go away. But at least now Brit will look down on me and know I tried. I tried to make it better."

When Dylan is done, he looks at me expectantly.

"I don't know what you want me to say," I answer.

"Say you forgive me. If you forgive me, maybe Brit does too."

I shake my head. "I don't. And she wouldn't either."

"Then say you'll try."

"I won't."

Dylan sighs. He reaches up to rub his hands through his hair, but the cuffs get caught on the tip of his nose, and he drops his hands in his lap again.

"Will you write to me?" Dylan asks. He doesn't look at me this time.

I shake my head again. "No. We won't be seeing each other again, or speaking. This is the end."

Dylan holds his hands over his mouth. He blinks out tears and nods, accepting the chapter of our lives together is over.

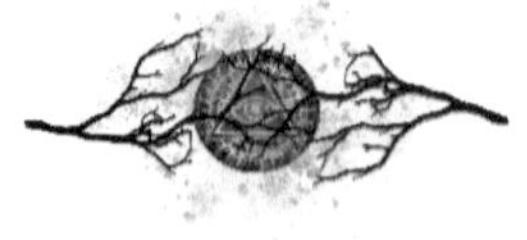

In my room, I slip beneath layers of blankets and shiver.

My heart aches, heavy and broken beneath my skin. A lump swells in my throat, but the tears don't come. I hate this part. The case is over; the culprit is caught, but the victims are still dead. There's no bringing them back just because I've connected all the puzzle pieces.

I turn over to face the door after a soft knock interrupts my thoughts. Our father stands in the doorway. He's back to looking polished and put together—a manilla folder in hand by his side. He doesn't breach the doorway, treating my room like the private sanctuary his office is.

"How are you?" he asks.

I sit up in bed and wrap blankets around my shoulders. "I'm alive." I shrug. "But that means a lot these days, huh?"

He gestures to the empty space at the foot of my bed. I nod, letting him in.

He sits, spine perfectly straight, and sets the file on the side of him I cannot see. "There were many victims of Sheriff Barrett. There won't be any more."

"If that's supposed to make me feel better, it doesn't." I lower my head, resting my chin against my chest. It should. I know that. I'm supposed to cheer and dance, or at least smile, knowing I stopped a monster from further damage. But I've never been good at the part after—the celebration part.

"There was no way you would have been able to save any of them," our father says. "These murders were months old. Some were years. Well hidden."

I try to swallow the regret clogging my throat, but it stays. "If I had seen them before I left..." my sentence trails off. What would I have done? I was taking on too much at the time. I was trying to solve murders, disappearances, robberies gone violent. I couldn't have added anything more to my full plate. I would have had a breakdown much faster. I still would have been sent away. The thought sits me upright to meet our father's eyes. It would be easy to place the blame on him to rid myself of the overwhelming guilt.

"If I hadn't sent you away?"

I suddenly understand, see, where John gets his composure from. With my brother, I find this personality endearing, quirky, just so John. With our father, however, I'm irritated. I want to know what he thinks of the situation, of me. I want to read expressions on his face like he can so easily read from mine.

Our father sighs, giving me a sliver of insight into his feelings. "If I hadn't sent you away, you may not be here today. May not have brought justice to those girls, to Brittany Hill."

I look away before he can see the tears stinging my red-rimmed eyes once more. I hate to admit it to myself, but he's right. If I had stuck around town after my breakdown, after my attempt, would I have kept trying to die again the moment I was alone without supervision? One thing is for sure: I would have been too overwhelmed to take on this case, pick apart these visions. I needed a break. I needed to clear my head.

"Delilah," our father says gently. I look at him again. "I would like to apologize."

My thoughts stop their spiral mid swirl, the worries and fears dissipating like a tornado without any more havoc to wreak.

"The way I've handled your abilities has been horrendous," he continues. Despite being more well-versed in stoic expression than his son, I can pinpoint the moment guilt replaces his masked face. The corners of his lips curl downward ever so slightly.

"I saw you as a gift for myself, for my career." He looks away now, blinking at the window. "You are more than your gifts. You are a person. I should have seen you that way before, and I didn't."

He looks back at me. "I am so very sorry for that, and I wish to rectify it."

All words leave my brain but one, so all I say is, "okay."

"Furthermore," he says, "I am proud of you."

I blink in surprise, dropping the blankets from around my shoulders. I didn't know the word 'proud' was in our father's vocabulary until now. And when he did eventually learn that word, I assumed it would be meant for John. Conner, perhaps. But not me. Never me.

Our father stands and extends the manilla file to me. "If you'd like to stop, no longer investigate your visions, I will understand. I will support you. I will still be proud of you."

I take the folder from his hands. Our father's small, tidy scrawl marks the tab that sticks out. It's dated three days ago followed by the last name *Peterson.*

"If you'd like to continue, I will help as needed, when needed. I will support you. I will remain proud of you."

I open the folder. There are pictures in here with sticky notes covering the images. Looping cursive labels the notes as victim one, victim two, and victim three. The fine line of his writing warns me these images are brutal—not to look unless necessary. I sift through the file as our father leaves the room.

I look up when my brothers enter and sit on either side of the bed.

"What was that about?" Conner asks, peering over my shoulder to read a police report on a possible serial murderer a county over.

John takes the covered up pictures and raises the yellow flaps. "I believe a meteor is overdue for this planet. People like this don't deserve life."

I look back and forth at my brothers. My co-investigators. My best friends. "You up for another case?"

Thank you for reading Clairvoyant. If you enjoyed the story, please leave a review on Amazon, Goodreads, or wherever else you leave reviews. It helps independent authors like me get the word out about their book.

Acknowledgements

There are so many people that helped make Clairvoyant the story it is.

Thank you to my husband for brainstorming with me at two in the morning, and reading dialogue aloud with me to make sure it sounded just right. I owe you an even bigger thank you for formatting all my work to save me from that headache.

Thank you to my parents for encouraging me and sharing your excitement for every story idea I come up with.

Thank you to my family and friends for reading my books and sharing all my Instagram, TikTok, and Facebook posts to new readers.

Thank you to my amazing critique partners and my editor for your feedback, and for hyping me up when I needed it.

Finally, I'd like to thank you, reader. Thank you for taking the time to read Clairvoyant and investigate the visions alongside the Dufort siblings. Don't worry about missing them too much—there are plenty more cases to solve.

About the Author

Born in Las Vegas, Samantha Alis has always dreamed of working with novels either through publishing her own or editing others'. She is currently working on stories that feature darker themes, spooky settings, and plenty of moral dilemmas. She published her first novel The Montgomery Estate in September 2024. When she's not writing, Samantha can be found watching horror movies, playing video games, or reading any book she comes across. She now lives in Quebec, Canada with her French Canadian husband.

You can find her website at: https://authorsamanthaalis.my.canva.site/